THE TOMAHAWK

Ben Castle was fresh out of prison when he arrived in Kearneyville to start over—and got involved in a stage-robbery and a murder. What was worse, he knew who the robber and killer was—an old friend. For reasons of his own Ben decided to go after him and walked straight into a trap. The 'old friend' was in cahoots with the rangeboss of the Tomahawk outfit and Ben knew too much about their set-up to stay alive.

THE TOMAHAWK

Buck Bradshaw

A Lythway Book

CHIVERS PRESS

BATH

First published in Great Britain 1986
by
Robert Hale Limited
This Large Print edition published by
Chivers Press
by arrangement with
Robert Hale Limited
1988

ISBN 0 7451 0679 X

British Library Cataloguing in Publication Data

Bradshaw, Buck
  The tomahawk.—(A Lythway book).
  I. Title
  823'.914[F]   PR6052.R26/

  ISBN 0–7451–0679–X

THE TOMAHAWK

CHAPTER ONE

A LONG WAY SOUTH

Ben Castle was a man who did not make excuses, not to others and not to himself. He served six years of an eight-year sentence for stage-robbery at the Canon City prison, walked out with two years remitted for good behaviour, caught the south-bound stage in the dusk of an early summer evening and lighted a stogie, the first tobacco he had savoured in six years.

The air smelled sweeter, the stars seemed more diamond-like and the flowing, uneven run of country he watched until darkness arrived, left Ben Castle with the nostalgic sensation of someone who was coming home, although he did not know this particular area, and in fact was not going home.

Being free was fine, but *feeling* free was better. He let the cigar die, rolled with the pitch and yaw of the old stagecoach, and ignored the man and woman opposite him who occasionally flicked glances in his direction.

Ben Castle was nearing forty with a sprinkling of grey at the temples. He was neither tall nor short, but medium sized, hard as rock from six years of manual labour, had light brown eyes and black hair. He was a strong-looking rather than a good-looking man.

The coach stopped at Beaverton to change horses. Ben and the other two passengers went inside for supper, and afterwards when they were on their way again, Ben lighted another cigar.

He was a Montanan. That was where he had committed his crime. He had no family to return to, few friends who would still be up there, and no reason to go back. He had worked all that out over the years. His intention was to go to southern Colorado, hire on as a tophand, which was what he had been before his one-time fling at outlawry, and start fresh. Six years out of a man's life was nothing to consider lightly, especially when he was no longer younger, but on the other hand if there was reason for bitterness over those wasted years, he had also come to the conclusion while back at Canon City, that the wisest course was to turn his back on all that, not dwell upon it, because he had associated with other inmates to whom bitterness had come to fill their unhappy lives behind bars and they had become mean, bleak, hating individuals. He was not going to be like that.

He had never tried to pass off his personal guilt to society, to his hard upbringing or to anything else. As he had once told Bill Ames, his best friend in prison, no one had shoved that gun in his hand, nor helped roll down the rocks

2

to block the road, and no one had forced him to take the bullion box.

By ten o'clock it was so cold the couple spread their buffalo robe and sat close beneath it. Ben Castle watched the stars, smelled the changing fragrances, first pines, then sage, then wildflowers, saw the faint lights of little towns come out of the moonless night, listened to the cadence of the horses, rode with the swing of the vehicle, and did not object to the chill at all. Free air, even if it was cold, was something to cherish.

They halted close to midnight at a sod-roofed old long and low log structure that looked more like an old fort than a way-station, and here the horses were changed again, and a new driver took over. He was a lanky, rawboned man with a drooping moustache who wore gauntlets of smoke-tanned buckskin. His whip had sterling silver ferrules. Ben smiled to himself. This one was an epitome of what small boys thought every stager should be. The only thing he lacked was the ivory-handled sixgun and fringes on his jacket. When they were ready to roll the driver climbed to his seat with a carbine and a shotgun, which he arrayed carefully in the boot. He barely glanced down to make certain his passengers were aboard then whistled up the hitch.

Ben braced for the lunge and the lurch, but there was none; Wild Bill, or whatever his name

3

was up there on the high seats was a good driver. He favoured the horses, seemed able to sense hog-wallows in the roadway in time to avoid them, and never once applied his binders. Ben's ironic thoughts about the man were diluted by his respect for the driver's finesse. Most stagers were converted freighters and drove like they were.

He slept, wakened when the gun-holster he was not supposed to be wearing as a former felon gouged his side, shifted the thing and went back to sleep.

Cold stiffened his joints toward morning. He awakened, saw the man and woman huddled under their robe studying him, turned to watch pearly dawn come slowly, and raised a hand to feel his bristly jaw. He had no idea where he was, but it was a clean, open country with the smell of newness to it. He guessed they had covered close to a hundred miles, and if his calculations were correct they should reach Kearneyville about mid-morning. All he knew about Kearneyville was that it had been named for a soldier, was in the heart of good livestock country, and had four roads going into it, and going out of it. He had studied the same old map for the last two years of his imprisonment before deciding on starting over down there. Everything he knew about the place had come from that old map.

The stager wheeled off the road at a turn-out

4

to rest and water his animals. The fact that his passengers now had an opportunity to climb out and get the kinks out of their joints did not seem to interest him at all. He did not even look back; he remained up front near the stone trough from which he carried water to the animals in a collapsible canvas bucket.

Ben strolled up to offer a hand. The rawboned man eyed him indifferently and handed him a bucket. Not a word was said after that until they had finished and the buckets had been stowed in the rear boot, then the lanky man lit a stogie, offered Ben one, held the match, and leaned upon his stage as he said, 'I guess you got out early. If you escaped you wouldn't be riding coaches out in the open would you?'

Ben gazed at the grey ash before replying. That he had been recognised was a shock, and a surprise; but most of all, if the stager knew him, and they were both going to the same town—well—civic-minded people talked, and what that meant was that he would not be able to start over down at Kearneyville after all.

He looked up, but the lanky man was gazing out where the pale sky was brightening toward sunup, ignoring Ben Castle. As though having read his passenger's mind and without looking around, he said, 'I guess six years is long enough, anyway . . . Well; we're runnin' ahead of schedule, but you never can tell with these

5

old rigs, so we might as well move out, Mister Castle.'

Ben said, 'Just a minute.'

The stager flicked ash and faced around, his rather hawkish, bronzed face calm and speculative. 'That was my brother's stage you stopped in Montana. Otherwise I wouldn't have recognised you. I followed the case in the newspapers. You got eight years. This is the sixth year.'

'Do you live in Kearneyville?' Ben asked, and got a nod of the stager's head by way of reply.

'Lived there for nine years now. Is that where you're going?'

Ben dropped the cigar and stepped on it. 'Yeah. Well, I was, but now I guess not.' He looked up. 'You ready to roll?'

The stager's dead-calm, steady grey eyes remained on Castle. 'Yeah, I'm ready. You didn't escape, did you?'

'No. I got two years shaved off for staying out of trouble.'

'Kearneyville's good stock country, the town is nice, folks are decent. You could do a hell of a lot worse.'

'Not with you living down there,' stated Ben.

The lanky man's lips lifted in a scanty smile. 'Mister, you did your time. What happened six years ago don't mean anything. It's what you do from here on. Hell, you'd be surprised at the secrets I got locked inside.' The driver was

6

turning when he said, 'I never talk about what I know about people, Mister Castle . . . let's roll.'

By the time the sun was climbing and all the dawn cold was past they had Kearneyville's rooftops in sight, the whip dropped down to a slogging walk for the last couple of miles in order to have his horses cooled-out when they reached town, and the man and woman had rolled their buffalo robe, fidgeted a little impatiently, and for the first time in almost twenty hours the man spoke to Ben Castle.

'If they ever build a railroad out here I'd never ride one of these things again as long as I live.' He accompanied that observation with a smile, and although Ben Castle was not much of a smiling man, he grinned slightly because no one knew better than Ben did, that unless a person had a considerable distance to travel, and wanted to do it the quickest way, stagecoaches left a lot to be desired. But he did not speak.

Kearneyville had trees on both sides of the wide roadway, several brick-fronted buildings, an air of thriving permanency, and in mid-morning had quite a bit of activity. There was a freight rig out front of the general store, rangemen on horseback as well as town-folk, mostly women in bonnets, on both sides of the road. Where they wheeled up into the Kearneyville corralyard, town loafers standing

7

idly in shade consulted their pocket watches and spoke among themselves, then they craned to see who the passengers were. They did not know the passengers, but this was the high-point of their mornings, exactly as the arrival of the north-bound coach from down south was the high-point of their late afternoons, and they would not know those passengers either.

Ben stretched, got his warbag and went out front. He knew where the boardinghouse was, even knew its name without ever having seen it before. He started up there.

An hour later, bathed and hungry, he went over to the cafe, was fed, went diagonally opposite to the tonsorial parlour for a shave and a shearing, listened to the running line of gossip among the shop's patrons, and strolled the town.

Kearneyville was, as the stager had said, a nice town, thriving, clean, folks nodded and spoke which meant it was also a friendly place, and when Ben was leaning out front of the harness works the rawboned stager ambled up and said, 'How does it strike you?'

Ben nodded. 'About like you said. Nice place.'

The stager had those elegant grey gauntlets tucked under his shellbelt. He stood a moment gazing up and down the roadway, then said, 'My name is Abraham Liston. Since I was a young buck folks have called me Horseshoe.' Liston continued to gaze among the buildings as he spoke. It appeared to be a characteristic of his to do this while speaking to people. 'I got that name because I used to chew horseshoe cut plug.'

Ben, who had never mastered the art of chewing tobacco, said, 'You still chew?'

'No. Just a cigar now and then.' Liston turned. 'Don't worry. You're a hell of a distance from Montana—or Canon City . . . Good luck.'

Ben turned to watch the lanky man stride southward. He was inclined to trust Horseshoe Liston. There was no reason for him to mention around town who Ben Castle was, unless he was a gossip, and if there was one thing Liston did not impress Ben as being, that was it.

The harness-maker walked out from under the overhang wearing a stained old brown apron. He was an older man with shrewd pale eyes, tobacco stains in his beard, and thick, work-scarred hands. He stood upon the edge of the duckboards and breathed deeply of the clean air. Then he said, 'If it'll just rain now and then, friend, this here'll be another good grass year.'

Ben grinned to himself. He was indeed in cattle country. Even town-folk talked in terms of what meant prosperity for them too.

He dryly said, 'It always has,' and the older

man looked at him, then laughed.

The heat was increasing when Ben ate his noon meal, then went up to the saloon, which was nearly empty, had a glass of beer, his first in a long time, and leaned on the bar enjoying the bite and scent of good home brew.

The barman was round-faced, had thin hair which he combed in a swirling cowlick in front, and offered Ben a newpaper to go with his beer.

It was a friendly town, for a fact.

CHAPTER TWO

A SHOCK

Ben no longer owned a saddle, and he wanted to make a leisurely excursion over this new country anyway, so he hired a nice little top-buggy with yellow running gear, and drove the big stud-necked Morgan mare east of town across pure livestock country.

It was early. The dew was gone but so far the day was cool and pleasant. He saw a few scattered bands of cattle, and once he watched someone's loose-stock raise dust at sight of his buggy.

The land was vast, gently rolling, and at this time of year had stirrup-high feed which in another couple of months would be heading up, starting to cure on the stalk. His practised eye told him the Kearneyville range country was not over-grazed, perhaps because there was so much of it, and perhaps because there did not appear to be many cow outfits. At least he only saw two sets of ranch buildings, both at a considerable distance.

A man whose background was solidly livestock since his teens approved of a territory which had not been allowed to get cluttered with stump-ranches and homesteads.

By mid-afternoon he had seen enough of the easterly country. In the morning he thought he would explore westward, but he was becoming quite satisfied with what he had seen so far.

The cafeman nodded when Ben walked in for his evening feeding, and up at the saloon the old harness-maker, without his apron, also nodded when Ben settled against the bar for a drink.

He got another newspaper, took it to a chair over where the ceiling light was best, sat down and read about a number of things which did not affect him at all, but which were interesting. For example the steam cars had built lines south and west of Denver, William Seward, Lincoln's Secretary of State, had died, the Germans were at war with the French, or at least had been when the newspaper had been published, but because newspapers were something of a rarity in cow country, and were usually long out of date by the time they

11

reached a place like Kearneyville, perhaps that particular war had been resolved by now.

A thick, heavy shadow blocked part of the light and Ben lowered his paper slightly to glance up. The man regarding him was big, not just tall and thick-through, but big in the sense that his hands and arms and legs were heavy and oaken. There was a walnut-stocked sixgun in his hip holster, a dull badge on his shirt-front, and a pair of riding gloves folded under his shellbelt. He had heavy features, very direct, piercing dark blue eyes, and a mouth like a beartrap. He pulled out a chair, sat down and without smiling, said, 'My name is Curtis Shelby . . . Sheriff of Ute County. You'll be Mister Castle.'

Ben's belly squeezed up a little as he nodded and leaned to put the newspaper on the table between them. 'Ben Castle,' he said.

The piercing blue eyes did not blink. 'Just out of curiosity, Mister Castle, I'd like to know where you was today.'

Ben answered forthrightly. 'Hired a rig and went driving out over the country east of town . . . Why?'

'Well; you're a stranger in town. I'm always interested in strangers, Mister Castle. Real interested today, because someone stopped a payroll stage on the west road.'

Ben's heart sank. Unless Horseshoe Liston had told this bear-built lawman who he was . . .

12

He said, 'Robbed it, Sheriff?'

'Clean as a whistle, Mister Castle. There's a silver mine west of town about sixty miles. They got their own little community over there. They have payday once a month. It would have been day after tomorrow, you see, except that someone robbed the money off that payroll stagecoach.'

Ben let his breath out in a long, silent sweep. 'I was east of town, Sheriff . . . I guess being a stranger and all, you'd wonder though.'

'I would for a fact, Mister Castle. Do you recollect anyone seeing you on the east range; or maybe you stopped and talked to someone?'

'I didn't see a soul, Sheriff.'

'You was just buggy-riding?'

'Yes sir. Just buggy-riding. I like this town and this country. A man's got to settle down some time, don't he?'

The large man gravely nodded his head. Then he said, 'You ride for a living, do you?'

'Yes.'

Curtis Shelby leaned back and relaxed in his chair. 'Mind telling me where you've worked in Colorado, Mister Castle?'

The only place Ben had worked in Colorado was at the Canon City prison. 'I'm from Montana,' he replied. 'I've never hired out down here. But that's my idea.'

'When you run out of money?'

Ben's uneasiness was getting mixed with

13

annoyance. 'Yes. Maybe before I run out of money, which may not be too long . . . Sheriff, mind telling me about the holdup?'

The barman came and waited impassively until Sheriff Shelby shook his head, then as the barman retreated Shelby said, 'It was one highwayman. He got the mail pouch which had the payroll in it.'

'How far from town?'

'Not very far. Maybe six or seven miles.'

Ben wagged his head. 'My buggy-riding didn't take me over in that direction.'

Sheriff Liston went speaking as though he had not heard. 'He shot the driver.'

Ben returned the larger man's gaze. 'Killed him?'

Not quite. He's over at Doc Crane's place. Maybe he'll make it and just as likely he won't. He's sort of a legend in these parts, Mister Castle. He scouted for the army years back. He hunted with the redskins, freighted, rode for Tomahawk—a big outfit northeast of town—and they say he's one of the best whips that ever came down the line.'

Ben's eyes widened. 'What's his name, Sheriff?'

As the lawman started to reply he placed both huge paws on the arms of the chair to shove upwards with. 'Horseshoe Liston . . . Take a little stroll with me, Mister Castle.'

Ben arose. 'Where to?'

14

'Doctor Crane's place at the upper end of town across the road . . . Horseshoe asked if you were still in town before he went into a coma.'

They left the saloon together, followed by a lot of eyes whose interest, and curiosity, had been aroused by the lengthy conversation between the local lawman and the stranger. It was already being rumoured around Kearneyville that there had been a stage robbery, but so far that was about all anyone knew.

Ben walked with his head down, silent until they reached a little picket fence out front of a cottage set back a short distance from the roadway. He halted near the gate and considered his companion. 'What did Horseshoe say about me, Sheriff?'

'Nothing. Just asked if you were in town.' Liston held the gate ajar for Ben to precede him toward the porch. When they reached it and he had a big fist raised to knock he also said, 'You two must have known one another from somewhere, Mister Castle. Otherwise Horseshoe wouldn't have asked about you, would he? But that don't interest me as much as him asking if you was in town.'

If Curtis Shelby had been about to say more, he did not have the opportunity. A tall, gaunt, slightly stooped older man with thin grey hair and a beak of a nose opened the door and

15

looked from Shelby to Ben Castle, then held the door wider for them to enter as he said, 'You found him, eh, Curtis?'

Shelby did not reply to the question as he introduced them. Doctor Crane was appropriately named. He really resembled a crane. He looked down at Ben from two blue eyes pulled in a little close on each side of his big beak of a nose. Without speaking, he nodded his head and led the way to a side room of his house, and just outside the closed door he glanced again at Ben Castle.

'He comes and goes, sometimes lucid, sometimes not. If he's not when we go in, we won't stay.'

Ben had one question. 'How bad off is he?'

'He got shot through the body up high. There's some bone damage but I don't expect to try and do much about that until I know he's going to make it. My worry right along has been internal bleeding. No way much to tell about that for a certainty.'

Doctor Crane opened the door and peeked in, then opened it wider and stepped through followed by Ben and the big lawman.

Horseshoe Liston looked deathly grey under his perpetual weathered tan. His eyes were open. They moved to Ben and remained there. He made no attempt to speak.

The sheriff stepped ahead and leaned. 'What did he look like, Horseshoe?'

16

The man in the bed continued to gaze at Ben, acting as though the sheriff had not spoken.

Doctor Crane hovered, clearly solicitous about the welfare of his patient. Ben ignored them both, stepped to the bedside and gently shook his head while his eyes and those of the wounded man were locked.

Liston slowly lowered his eyelids. He had neither spoken nor moved since the arrival of his visitors, and now he appeared oblivious to their presence. Doctor Crane herded them out of the room on tiptoes, took them all the way to the parlour then ignored Ben to say, 'It's not very hopeful, Curtis.'

The large sheriff looked down, then raised his head. 'Is there something you could give him, John, to make him come round even for a little while? He had to have seen the highwayman. If he dies without saying anything I don't think there's goin' to be much I can do . . . Maybe get him around for just five or ten minutes?'

Doctor Crane pursed his lips. It was not the request which bothered him, it was the ignorance of it. 'Nothing,' he said a trifle irritably. 'Stimulants would perhaps do it. And without much doubt they would also kill him.'

Sheriff Liston preceded Ben out onto the porch, and when Doctor Crane had closed the door after them, the sheriff looked balefully at his companion. 'Where did you two know each

17

other?' he asked, his tone no longer carefully devoid of hardness.

Ben answered truthfully. 'On the stage down from Beaverton. I helped him water the horses and we talked a little.'

'That's all?'

'That's all, Sheriff.'

'Then why did he ask where you were right after they got him back here to town after he had been shot?'

Ben hung fire over replying while he did some private speculating. When he finally spoke all he said was: 'You'll have to ask him . . . Where, exactly, was that stage stopped?'

'I told you, about seven miles west of town.'

'Near something; a big tree, some rocks; how would I know the place?'

Curtis Shelby eyed his companion shrewdly. 'Why? You expect to go out there?'

'Yeah, something like that.'

Shelby's speculative gaze lingered before he eventually said, 'I'll take you out there, but we'll have to wait for morning because by the time we got out there today it'd be too dark to see anything . . . I was figuring on going out there tomorrow anyway.'

They strolled slowly southward on the west side of the road, past the harness works, the abstract office, a narrow little store that said 'Seamstress' over the door, and on down to a building Ben had noticed earlier, the Ute

18

County jailhouse. He had no desire to enter, but Curtis Shelby, who had always managed to be behind Ben a few steps, jerked with a thumb to indicate Ben was to go inside.

It was begining to look to Ben as though Sheriff Shelby was an individual who clung to an idea like a bulldog.

Ben took a rickety old chair near the door and watched Curtis Shelby go behind a large, untidy table and drop down into a chair with a squeaky steel spring beneath it. When the lawman was comfortable he said, 'Why, Mister Castle?'

Ben did not have to ask what the question was. He had already heard it at least three times. He used the same answer. 'You'll have to ask him, Sheriff.'

'You got a better answer, Mister Castle. It's not just that you and Horseshoe talked a little while watering some horse. Hell, he's shot darn near to death. A man like that don't just up and waste what little time he's got left asking if someone was in town, unless he's got a notion there was a connection between the man and him getting shot.'

Ben sighed, and did not allow this conversation to remain as it was. 'I thought this was about what you had in mind over at the saloon,' he stated. 'And I'll tell you something else. If you got a suspicion I robbed that payroll-stage and shot the driver, you're not just wrong as hell, but what's worse, Sheriff . . .

19

Horseshoe didn't see the man who shot him, whether they were up close or not. If he had, and if for some reason he thought I might have done it, he wouldn't have to ask whether I was in town or not, would he? Because he'd already have known I wasn't in town.'

The distraction worked, as it could reasonably have been expected to, because Ben had made a point which had not as yet occurred to the sheriff. He leaned on his unkempt table with both elbows planted hard down, and gradually drifted his gaze from Ben Castle to the cell-room door, which was thick oak studded with reinforcing big bolt-heads holding straps of more steel in place.

Ben shoved his hat back, regarded Shelby, and almost felt sorry for the large man. If this had been a case requiring brute strength, Curtis Shelby would not have had a bit of trouble. But it was not that kind of an affair. Ben studied the heavy jaw and the mighty shoulders.

He arose, finally, and said, 'What time, in the morning?'

Shelby grunted and also arose. 'Six. At the livery barn. I keep a couple of horses down there. We'll use my animals, and get an outfit from the liveryman . . . Castle, be there.'

Outside in the warmth Ben wagged his head.

Being warned to be at the liverybarn in the morning reinforced Ben's notion that Curtis Shelby was not another Alan Pinkerton; if he

20

had doubts about Ben still being in town come morning, instead of warning him not to leave town, he could have simply locked him up.

CHAPTER THREE

HORSESHOE

It was cool when they left town, the great flow of grassland was soft-shadowed with a faint haziness which seemed to increase as they rode on westward a number of miles. They had eaten at the cafe, and except for having exchanged a few grunts, they rode in preoccupied silence.

Ben had thought about several things last night in his bed up at the roominghouse. One of them was that Horseshoe Liston had evidently been able to talk when they had found him and fetched him back to Kearneyville, and although he had asked whether or not Ben had been in town, he had not mentioned what he knew about Ben. He had told Ben he would say nothing and he had kept his word, but if he had suspected that Ben might have been the man who shot him, would keeping his word go that far?

Maybe Liston was a fairer man than Ben knew he was. They were passing a deep erosion gully on the left side of the road when Ben said,

'Who brought Liston back to town?'

'A freighter named Harris who hauls between Kearneyville and some other towns west, and south, of here.'

'He was conscious?'

'Yes. He asked Harris to see whether a man named Ben Castle was in town.'

'I see. And that's where you got it—from Harris?'

'Yeah.'

Ben turned his head. 'What did the liveryman tell you?'

'That you'd rented a rig and drove east.'

'. . . You figure that was a ruse, maybe, and I cut around town and went west after his stagecoach?'

'Well, Mister Castle, in the first place, I hired a man to shag your wheel marks yesterday afternoon. They didn't cut around westerly. The marks went quite a distance out. It don't seem likely you could have driven that far, and still caught up with Horseshoe's stage. And there is another thing: Horseshoe left town on the payroll-stage a half-hour before you rented that rig and drove eastward. If you did it, I don't see how. Unless you got wings.'

'Anything else?'

'Yeah. You don't own a saddle horse and you didn't rent one. Maybe you could have borrowed one. The highwayman was riding a bay horse. But if you did, I'd sure like to know

22

what you did with him. You was driving a top-buggy.' Sheriff Shelby put a pair of shrewd, thoughtful eyes upon his companion.

'I don't see how, Mister Castle, but let me tell you for a fact that if you did it, I'll find out.'

When they arrived at the place where the robbery and shooting had taken place, Ben could have found it by himself without being told about the landmarks, which were simply two more of those erosion ditches, about a hundred yards apart, and a deep swale in the roadway, because there were deep scars where a driver had slammed on his binders and skidded the big rear wheels, then had half swung his rig crossways in the road.

There were other marks. The highwayman had been in the swale invisible to Horseshoe Liston until his coach had breasted the tip of the swale, and by then it was too late to do anything.

Curtis Shelby dismounted and quartered a lot, but Ben sat astride moving his horse a little to do the same thing. He only dismounted when he thought he had read the sign about right. Then he leaned across the saddle-seat studying the great emptiness of open country all around. The highwayman had chosen the only suitable spot in sight for his ambush, and it was a good site for something like stopping a stagecoach.

But how had he known all that money was on board?

When Shelby walked over Ben asked him about that. Shelby shrugged mighty shoulders. 'My guess is that he didn't know; that he got real lucky. What do you make out of the sign?'

'One man, Sheriff, riding a slightly pigeon-toed horse. If I was asked to guess, I'd say he came from the north.' Ben's gaze wandered in that direction. 'Back-tracking up in that direction through thick grass would make a man earn his keep, wouldn't it? Especially after a night has gone by.' He turned his attention back to Sheriff Shelby. 'How do things look to you?'

'There's no shell casing, which was what I specially wanted to find.'

'Maybe he picked it up, or maybe he didn't lever up another load after firing. Do you know for a fact he used a carbine and not a sixgun?'

'Doc Crane says it was a carbine bullet. If it had been a sixgun up close like that, it would have blown a hole in Horseshoe a man could shove his fist through . . . It was a Winchester, and afterwards he picked up the casing.'

'If he levered the gun, Sheriff.'

Shelby ignored the comment and stood a long time gazing at the broad wheel marks in the dusty roadway. After a while Ben interrupted his reverie with a question.

'Has this happened before, lately?'

Shelby shook his head. 'Only once since I been sheriff. About four years ago a couple of

24

buckaroos tried it. All they got for their trouble was a bale of polka-dot dress goods bound for the store in Kearneyville, and a crate of whisky for the saloon. And I ran them down with a ten-man posse and brought them back.'

'Sitting up or belly-down?'

Shelby's shrewd eyes showed irritation. 'Sitting up. But if either one of them had so much as reached up to scratch, I'd have shot them both.' Curtis Shelby turned toward his left stirrup. He had seen all he wanted to see, or at least all he could make any sense out of, and that did not include anything which might have helped him find the man who had shot Horseshoe and who had also stolen sixty thousand dollars, more than Curtis Shelby could imagine; more by thousands than he had ever seen in one lump sum.

Ben was still on the ground gazing out over the countryside when he asked about the area north and west. Shelby answered shortly. 'Just like what you see for a hundred miles or so, except northward where the mountains are.' He squinted in that direction. 'My guess is that he went back up there. It's the only decent cover. I figure he came down here in the dark, maybe an hour or two before daylight, and waited. Afterwards he went back into those darned mountains.'

They returned to town, arrived after dinner time, and when Ben finally got up to the cafe,

25

Shelby had already been there and gone, according to the cafeman.

They did not meet again until late evening, up at the saloon where Sheriff Shelby usually had a nightcap after making his final round of the day. Ben had been reading one of those old newspapers the barman kept around, but when Curtis Shelby walked over and sat down with a great sigh, Ben was leaning back, glass in his hand, staring steadily at the yonder wall, so lost in thought he did not realise someone had joined him at the table until the sheriff let go with that big sigh. Then he turned and impassively eyed the big man.

'You tracked him,' Ben said matter-of-factly, then awaited the answer.

Shelby had indeed been tracking the renegade. 'Like I said, he went northward to the mountains.'

Ben cocked an eyebrow. 'That's one hell of a long ride, Sheriff.'

'Well . . . I didn't go all the way. If I had I'd never have got back to town in time for supper. But I shagged his tracks for three hours and they never even swerved from a straight line to the mountains.' Sheriff Shelby looked up when the barman brought a bottle and a glass, then pushed them aside and leaned to say, 'Sixty thousand dollars . . . When I rode in this evenin' one of the head honchos from the mine was waiting at the office for me . . . He was mad.'

Ben could understand that.

Shelby tipped the bottle carefully, tipped it back and reached for the shot-glass. 'The best I could tell him was that we're working on it.' He lifted the glass, reared his head back and dropped the whisky straight down, just as Ben Castle spoke with a slight frown.

'*We* are working on it?'

Shelby shuddered, blew out a breath and slid the empty glass over beside the bottle. He looked straight at Ben and said, 'You and me.'

For a while Ben sat relaxed gazing at the big lawman, then his gaze drifted over along the bar where several dusty rangemen were lining up, beating pantsleg with their hats and teasing the barman.

Shelby brought his attention back with another statement. 'I wrote a letter to the mine company's head office for the name of the bank they got that money from.'

Ben said, 'What for?'

'For serial numbers and whatnot.'

Ben snorted. 'You been readin' penny-dreadfuls, Sheriff. It won't matter what the serial numbers were. He got that money yesterday morning. That's a full two days ago. By now he's down in New Mexico on his way over the border, or somewhere else, just as far. Serial numbers aren't going to help find him.'

Shelby was a dogged man. 'I told you, he

rode northward into the mountains, in the opposite direction from New Mexico.'

Ben was not impressed. His point had not been New Mexico in particular, it had been that the renegade now had a two-day start. By morning he would be so far away . . .

Doctor Crane walked over, gravely pulled out a chair and dropped down upon it, eyed the whisky bottle a long time, then through sheer will power looked away from it without reaching. He had something else on his mind.

Ben was watching the medical practitioner. So was Curtis Shelby. Neither of them offered any openers, so it was up to John Crane, and he did not procrastinate, because he had been seeking the sheriff for just this meeting. He said, 'Horseshoe cashed in this afternoon. I'm surprised he hung on as long as he did.' Doctor Crane's gaze drifted back to the bottle with the little sticky glass beside it, then drifted away again. 'I'll open him up tomorrow and see what happened, then you can plant him, Curtis.' Now, finally, Crane's long, narrow hand snaked toward the whisky.

Ben did not especially like what he had just heard. 'Why open him up? He's dead, isn't he? We know what killed him—someone's carbine bullet. What's performing an autopsy going to prove we don't already know?'

Crane downed a jolt, and immediately colour came to his face, his eyes brightened, and he

28

answered Ben Castle in a firm voice. '*You* are satisfied, but I'm a medical man. I'd like to know exactly how much damage was done inside him.'

Ben sat looking at the long, scrawny man without speaking. Curtis Shelby had taken no part in the discussion. He had been thinking. Now, he said, 'John, by any chance did Horseshoe say anything before he died?'

He had, but Doctor Crane had another drink before speaking. He was clearly one of those individuals to whom just one drink was almost enough, and to whom two drinks were almost too much. He considered the big lawman with sparkling eyes. 'He was rational for a short while this morning. Looked better and told me he felt a lot better.' Doctor Crane shrugged birdlike bony shoulders. 'It happens like that, sometimes. It's like they all of a sudden get a big surge of energy . . . When it peters out, they got nothing left.'

Curtis was polite but impatient. 'I guess that might be so, John . . . What did he talk about?'

Crane clasped both hands atop the table and leaned a little, regarding them. 'He said he never saw the highwayman before that he could recollect; said he was a stocky man with sandy hair, dark eyes, maybe forty to forty-five, and had a scar on one hand, sort of like a burn-scar. Not very large and sort of shiny . . . Horseshoe said when this feller stopped him and took the

29

pouch he was wearing gloves. After he got the pouch he stepped away, raised the Winchester and shot. Horseshoe said it knocked him off the seat into the front boot. He was bleedin' and dazed—was just hangin' there and this feller walked over pullin' off his gloves, to see if Horseshoe was dead. He must have figured he was, because he lowered his carbine and turned away . . . That was when Horseshoe saw the scar on the back of his hand.'

Sheriff Shelby sat like a big gorilla filling his chair, gazing at John Crane in silence. Ben Castle straightened up and reached for the bottle.

Doctor Crane had said what he had arrived to say. He had also downed his share of whisky; more than his share, actually, because for some intolerable reason his body chemistry prevented him from drinking except very rarely, and in very small amounts. He eyed the bottle, then lifted his eyes to Sheriff Shelby. 'Well . . . ?'

'I'll have the tinker make a box in the morning. We'll bury him tomorrow afternoon. I'll catch the parson first thing before he leaves town on one of his missions.' Shelby paused, then added a little more. 'I don't know what he had, except for that whip with the silver ferrules and his weapons, but I'll talk to the corralyard boss in the morning. You'll get paid, John, as soon as I can auction off his stuff.'

Doctor Crane left the table, set a course in

30

the direction of the spindle doors, hitched up his shoulders and walked steadily across the room without looking left or right.

Curtis Shelby saw Ben watching, and explained. 'He can't handle liquor. Not even dribbles of the stuff. Right now he's bein' dignified. He don't ever want folks to know when he's drunk.' The sheriff cast a casual look over where Crane was pushing past the doors. 'Everyone knows. Look at how he walks. It's a dead give-away.'

He faced around as Ben put both hands atop the table, palms down, and said, 'Now you can quit worryin' that maybe I did it.'

Curtis Shelby wagged his head. 'You weren't listening out yonder, were you? I told you why I didn't see how you could have done it.' His eyes dropped to the thick, work-hardened hands.

CHAPTER FOUR

A LONG DAY

Ben had a riddle which he took to bed with him, and the only person who could have resolved it was dead. But Ben also had a fair idea about his riddle.

The reason Horseshoe Liston had wanted to know whether Ben was in town, even though he

31

had known it had not been Ben who had robbed and shot him, was that Horseshoe had known that Ben Castle had been a highwayman. What seemed clear to Ben, now, was that Horseshoe had thought he might have been an accomplice to the man who had robbed, and shot, him. That was why he had wanted to know whether Ben had been in town or not, because if he had not, then he would have been lying out there somewhere with a cocked carbine, giving the other highwayman cover. But he had been in town. When Horseshoe had been convinced of that, he had died without saying anything to incriminate Ben Castle.

Ben lay in the cool stillness of his room gazing out the south-wall window straight down Kearneyville's wide, dusty main roadway. It was empty, there were only a few lights still burning.

He knew who had taken the money pouch and had shot Horseshoe Liston. He had known it even before Doctor Crane had appeared at the saloon. There had been a small item in the newspaper he had been reading when Curtis Shelby had walked up. It had not been positive proof, but it had been enough for Ben. Then Crane had arrived. What he'd said had clinched it. Ben was absolutely certain he knew the identity of the man who had stopped that payroll-stage.

When sleep eventually arrived he was still

32

struggling with his thoughts. He liked Kearneyville, the countryside round about, and the people. The moment he identified Liston's killer he would have to leave, start a fresh search for a place he could settle down in.

If he didn't identify the renegade, Horseshoe, who had befriended Ben and who had kept his word to him, would go into the ground, a casualty of a man who would do that same thing again, sooner or later.

When morning arrived Ben felt more tired than when he had gone to bed last night. He was the first diner at the cafe, only grunted when the friendly cafeman tried to strike up a conversation, and was down at the livery barn renting a saddle animal about the time Sheriff Shelby sat down at Ben's vacated place in the cafe.

He left town by riding up the west-side alley unobserved, and when he was a couple of miles out he began riding in a diagonal manner to intercept those tracks Curtis Shelby had followed for a few miles yesterday.

They were not difficult to find. In summertime a horse's legs bent a lot of grass and his hooves trod it flat.

Ben was a good tracker although in this case he was not required to be. He loped a couple of extra miles, sank to a walk when he was close enough to the mountains and their foothills to be able to make out small details and, up there, the trampled grass abruptly stopped going northward.

Ben halted, rolled and lit a smoke, glanced back down where he had seen the last of Sheriff Shelby's marks, then squared up gazing eastward, the direction the tracks went from this point.

The highwayman had not gone up into the mountains.

Ben settled into a lope for another couple of miles, until he crested out atop a long, gradual rise of land where heat-haze was just beginning to dull-out the clear sharpness of the day.

There was a large ranch yard up ahead a couple of miles. It had big trees, a number of scattered log outbuildings, a weathered old set of pole working-corrals, and a main-house also of logs, which was large with a veranda completely around it to keep snow and rain off in winter, and heat off in summertime.

It was obviously the headquarters of a big ranch, and even at that distance Ben had no difficulty recognising the signs of efficiency and prosperity. Whoever owned that place was established, and probably well off.

But that was what he saw and recognised, it was not why he had followed those tracks.

He turned back down off the landswell, aimed for some southward creek-willows, and when he reached water he tanked up the livery horse, loosened the rigging, and as the grateful animal grazed, Ben sat like an old bronco-Indian with his carcass in shade, his hatbrim pulled low, his tanned, strong features relaxed and pensive.

If what he thought was true, then he had been incorrect last night at the saloon; the highwayman who had murdered for the payroll pouch was *not* two hundred miles away and still riding.

He eventually arose, dusted off, snugged things up, stepped up astride and set a leisurely course in the direction of Kearneyville. He was no closer to his ultimate decision than he had been last night at the roominghouse. If he had not liked the countryside, the town, most of the people he had met in both, the decision would not have been hard at all, because regardless of other considerations, he had no use for murderers. He was convinced that the highwayman had not had to kill Liston. Once he had the damned pouch all he'd had to do was light out, as other highwaymen would have done.

Some men were just natural killers. Perhaps if Liston had not been willing to see that Ben got his chance . . . Naw—that was part of it, for a fact, but the decisive thing was that there had been no excuse for that shooting—except that the killer probably thought Liston could either identify him or at least give a good enough description for others to identify him, and even

35

those things were insufficient reason to shoot Horseshoe Liston in cold blood.

Dusk was on the way as Ben rode into the Kearneyville livery barn from the back alley, swung off and handed the reins to the hostler. He paid up for the use of the animal, and without saying a word, strode up the cool runway to emerge on Main Street.

He thought they had probably buried Horseshoe by now. At least that had been Sheriff Shelby's plan. As he folded his roping gloves under his shellbelt and started for the cafe, he saw two dozing horses at the tie-rack in front of the jailhouse. Under different circumstances he might have smiled, because if that was another pair of officials from that mine, Sheriff Selby was probably having his hide peeled off a little more.

The cafe had half a dozen men eating at the counter. The cafeman nodded at Ben, took his order, and went out back to fill it. A muscular older man who was eating barley soup with chunks of meat floating in its grease, looked around, nodded and said, 'That's a hell of a thing that happened to Abraham Liston . . . But maybe you didn't know him.'

'I knew him,' replied Ben, leaning back as the cafeman brought his meal.

The muscular man bailed out the last of his barley soup and shoved the bowl away. 'I guess I ought to be used to them, but I ain't. Funerals

36

depress me. If it's someone I knew pretty well, I have trouble shakin' it off for a while.'

Ben considered his meal. He had not eaten all day and should have been hungry. He picked up the utensils and went to work. The man at his side was leaning comfortably on the counter, evidently in no hurry to depart, and in need of someone to talk to. 'The son of a bitch got the mine's monthly payroll. That should have been enough, wouldn't you say?'

Ben nodded his head and continued to eat.

The muscular man sighed and reared back to arise. 'I'd like to get my hands around that outlaw's throat,' he said, stepping back, dropped some coins on the counter, nodded to Ben, and walked out.

The cafeman came to refill Ben's coffee cup and wagged his head. 'That there was Manuel Bent, town blacksmith. Him and Horseshoe Liston been playing pinochle at the saloon every Thursday night for about three years. You got to excuse him. He had tears runnin' down his face out at the cemetery this afternoon.'

Ben looked up. 'It's nothing to be ashamed of.'

The cafeman thought about that, then agreed with it. 'No. You're right.'

'Sheriff Shelby been in for his supper yet?'

'Naw. There's a couple of strangers over at the jailhouse with him. They come in here about two hours ago. A little early for supper,

37

but I fed them. I told them where they could most likely find the sheriff.'

Ben's upwards gaze was fixed upon the cafeman. 'Lawmen?'

'I'd guess that they was, yes, but neither of them had a badge showing . . . That's fresh-made berry pie, if you got room for it.'

Ben declined the pie, paid up and left the cafe. Out front, he leaned upon an overhang upright to make a smoke, and while lighting it he studied the pair of patiently-standing horses. They were good quality animals. They were rigged out with serviceable saddles and had bedrolls lashed above some of those capacious army-style saddlebags, the kind people used who travelled considerable distances.

He was turning away when the jailhouse door opened and three men emerged. The largest of the three was Sheriff Shelby, but the other two men were about as tall, younger, but not as thick and broad.

Ben turned southward and kept walking. When he finally halted down in front of the saddlery and looked back, Sheriff Shelby was holding the cafe door for the pair of lanky strangers to enter first.

When his smoke was finished, Ben returned to the livery barn for a while, killing time before he eventually headed for the roominghouse. He did not want to encounter the sheriff or his visitors.

He got a bar of tan soap and an old towel from the roominghouse proprietor and went out back, down a weed-grown little crooked pathway to the bath-house.

Later, dressed in his only clean change of clothing, and with nightfall full down, he decided against a nightcap at the saloon and sat in a rickety old cane-bottom chair on the roominghouse's wide, long porch.

Kearneyville's day-long activity had dwindled considerably. Ben watched the evening stage come up through town from the south, an hour behind schedule which was not unusual, and when it had passed a long-legged silhouette came toward the porch from the opposite side of the roadway.

Ben thought Doctor Crane would turn toward his cottage when he reached the near-side plankwalk. Instead, the big stooped figure came steadily forward. When John Crane had one foot on the edge of the porch he said, 'Good evening,' and came ahead to search for a chair.

Ben echoed the greeting. 'Good evening.'

Doctor Crane sat down, thrust out his long legs and leaned back to achieve the maximum comfort. He did not seem hurried nor anxious. Ben guessed he had recognised him on the porch and with nothing else to do, had stopped to visit for a while. 'Didn't see you at the funeral this afternoon,' the doctor said.

39

Ben answered truthfully. 'They don't help me very much, Doctor. I'm like the blacksmith—they put me down in the dumps for a few days.'

John Crane was understanding. 'They affected me that way when I was about your age, maybe a little younger . . . But at my trade you get over that, Mister Castle . . . I guess no one ever gets used to funerals though, not even someone like me who's been to dozens of them.' John Crane sat studying the man opposite him in the gloom. 'I finished my autopsy of Horseshoe this morning.'

Ben shifted in his chair and turned his head to look in a different direction.

'It was about as I figured. He was bleedin' inside. Not much though . . . But enough. Years back when I was a surgeon in the army there was another surgeon who'd open them up to tie it off or maybe cauterise it . . . I always thought he had the right idea. Trouble was, mostly what we had to work on during the war was men who were already cooling out . . . He saved a few though.'

Ben brought his eyes back slowly to Doctor Crane's dim face in the porch shadow. 'Nice night,' he said, with a faintly harsh sound to his voice which Doctor Crane did not miss.

'You care for a cigar, Mister Castle?'

Ben declined. 'No thanks. I'm not much of a smoker. Just now and then.'

Doctor Crane produced a long, thin stogie, lighted it, savoured the smoke with his head tilted back, and through a blue cloud of exhaled smoke he said, 'They thought you'd left the country.'

Ben frowned. 'Who thought that?'

'Curtis Shelby and that pair of federal marshals who rode in this afternoon.' Crane's head came down slowly. 'Curtis was looking for you. We met down in front of the general store, but I hadn't seen you since yesterday.' As he stopped speaking Doctor Crane drew on his cigar again, then sat in long silence gazing across the porch at Ben.

A number of thoughts crowded into Ben's mind. He sat a long while gazing southward down Main Street unconscious of Doctor Crane's unwavering gaze. Then Crane spoke again, softly and gently. 'I'll guess, if you want me to. Those federal men knew your name when Curtis told them you were helping him with the robbery and killing.'

Ben continued to gaze down the wide, dark roadway. Well hell; he was not going to have to make the decision after all. He was not going to be able to remain in the Kearneyville country.

It did not surprise him that federal marshals knew his name. Maybe, if he'd had sense enough to take another name—but he had chosen not to do that. Perhaps the reasons were not very good, but they had seemed good

41

enough at the time he made the decision.

He arose. 'I'll look the sheriff up in the morning, Doctor. Good night.'

CHAPTER FIVE

THE STALK

He did not look up Curtis Shelby in the morning. In fact before sunup he was no longer in Kearneyville, he was riding another livery horse northeastward through the pre-dawn chill in the direction of that big ranch he had seen yesterday, and he did not feel happy about what he intended to do.

He got out there on that landswell before sunrise, hunkered up there like an Indian with the reins to his drowsing horse in his hands, simply watching. He saw the first streamer of smoke rise above the cookhouse where the cook was making breakfast, and he watched a hatless, tow-headed man go among the corrals pitching meadow hay to the working-stock. He could see lights brighten among the buildings and, with the sun much closer, he watched a stocky person march from the main-house to the bunkhouse porch, confer with someone, and march back. He assumed that had been the owner giving his rangeboss orders for the day.

He saw all these things without being able to make out much in the way of details because of the distance, and the poor-to-fair visibility.

He continued to sit as the riders trooped over to be fed at the bunkhouse, and when they trooped back. He arose when they entered the barn to saddle up, and when the sun was first beginning to show over the eastern rims, Ben got astride, turned back down off the landswell for a short distance, then swung in the saddle and watched four riders head northwesterly out of the yard.

It was open country and full daylight was coming. They would see him out there if they held to their present course, so he rode over into the foothills.

What he had in mind did not require haste, it required patience, and Ben Castle had had six years to learn that particular virtue.

He picked an excellent hiding place for his horse and went up atop a gritty little round knoll where a couple of unhealthy-looking pine trees were struggling to survive where the soil was thin, shallow and rain-leached.

The rangemen were in no hurry. They were talking back and forth, a couple of them were smoking their first cigarettes of the day, and the bull-necked red-headed man who was in the lead seemed to be good-natured because a couple of times he laughed at what someone had said.

They skirted the foothills remaining in open, more or less flat country, unaware that a watcher was lying on his belly in speckled pine-shadows watching them very intently.

After they had passed by Ben went back down, got into the saddle and skulked in their wake, but kept the broken country on his left side so no one would see him. But the riders did not look back. They went another mile ahead, perhaps closer to a mile and a half, then the red-headed man gestured with a gloved hand and two horsemen swung down-country in the direction of some cattle which were about ant-size. Ben thought this was not a preliminary gather; there were too many cattle down yonder, and they were too strung out, for just two men to do much with them.

He rode a little closer to the edge of his foothills, which was risky, but he had to know who the rider was the red-headed man was taking with him.

He could not make a positive identification without getting much closer, but what he saw satisfied him, and when the red-headed man, who acted like a rangeboss, and his remaining rider rode westward again, at a leisurely walk, Ben faded deeper into the hills again, and followed them.

They halted at a cottonwood-spring, offered their horses water, which the animals were not interested in, and they stood in shade talking

44

for a long time before the red-headed man swung up and turned northward, up through the foothills, riding as though he knew where he was going in the slightly more distant, forested mountains.

Ben hid. He was too far back for the rangeboss to see him, as long as the rangeboss continued northward. He pushed through some thorn-bushes to see where the man at the cottonwood spring had got to. He was still down there with his horse.

That did not make much sense. If they were looking for cattle it would have been obvious that there was none anywhere near the cottonwood spring. A man could see in three directions for fifty miles, and so far the only critters had been southward, back yonder where the rangeboss had sent two of his riders.

But for that matter it did not make any sense for the rangeboss to ride up into the mountains either. His chances of finding cattle up where tree-resin soured the ground so that grass would not grow, and where the scent of cougars and bear was bound to frighten any kind of four-footed animals, were about as good as the chances of a snowball in hell.

Ben waited a while, watching the loafing man over in cottonwood shade. He was waiting for something, sure as hell. Whatever it was did not interest Ben as much as skulking close enough to verify his suspicion about that man interested him.

He took his time. There was underbrush, crumbly jumbles of grey stone, and the arroyo's winter runoff from the mountains which had been cutting deeper each year down through the foothills.

It was still early. The sun was climbing but thus far the day was pleasantly cool with almost limitless visibility and a faint but persistent fragrance of wildflowers.

Ben squatted in the underbrush studying the approaches to the spring, and that hip-shot man over there who was now building a smoke while his horse swished at flies, cropped grass, and stamped now and then as mosquitoes bothered him.

He sighed as he backed out of the underbrush, walked back until a low hill was between them, then slid down the crumbly bank of an erosion arroyo, and began walking back in the direction of the spring.

It was feeding time down in his arroyo for a number of varmints whose variety spanned quite a spectrum. Not only did he send a little grey-muzzled fox fleeing like the wind, but he also had to out-wait a couple of rattlesnakes. There were birds among the tangled undergrowth. When they recovered from surprise, they scolded Ben unmercifully; he was trespassing and they did not like that at all.

It was cooler in the arroyo until he got close

enough to see treetops then, as the arroyo tipped upwards slightly where sunshine could reach, it was warmer. It was also slightly soggy underfoot, perhaps because the spring seeped into this low place.

He set a course for the base of a flourishing, well-watered bush, reached it with mud beginning to cling to his boots, leaned against the crumbly bank and reached with one hand to very gently ease aside some of the thorny ground-level limbs.

The range rider was sitting, now, hat in the grass, either thinking or listening to his horse eating farther back. He was a lined, deeply tanned man who looked to be in his fifties. His hair was full on both sides, but thin on top. He had unusual eyes. They were light tan, like the eyes of a goat, and they also had a very slight tilt at their outer corners.

Ben eased the little limbs back into place, straightened back off the bank of soft soil, and stood a moment or two in solemn reflection.

Then he lifted out his Colt, ducked down to pass the flourishing bush, moved onwards until he knew that when he straightened up he would be visible from the waist up, and hesitated long enough to listen for sounds which he did not hear, then he eased straight up.

The relaxed range man did not see Ben at once, but his horse did, and snorted. The tan-eyed man pushed up off his leaning-tree to look

47

northward in the direction his companion had ridden—and saw Ben Castle gazing at him as though he had come up out of the ground. The man's astonishment was so great his tan eyes got steadily wider, to their limit, and his mouth fell open.

Ben raised his right hand with the gun in it, cocked the weapon and quietly said, 'Nice seein' you again, Bill. I read in a newspaper that you had escaped . . . Toss your gun away.'

The range man did not move for a long time. Evidently his astonishment had been the kind that paralysed people.

Ben got out of the arroyo and went a little closer, then repeated what he had said earlier. 'Shed the gun, Bill. Toss it away in the grass . . . Bill, I'm not a ghost. Now toss that gun away!'

Finally, the seated man lifted out his Colt and gave it a little toss as though his action was unimportant. He spoke as he did this. 'Ben! Where in the hell did you come from? I had a notion you was goin' out to California when you got out.'

Castle holstered his gun, squatted down in shade, shoved back his hat and eyed the other man without saying a word for a long time. Then all he said was, 'Why did you kill him, Bill? You got the payroll pouch. There was no call to shoot the driver too.'

Those tan eyes slowly assumed a crafty

48

expression. The man was no longer surprised. 'What are you talking about? Where in hell was you, Ben?'

Castle picked up a twig and began methodically to scrap adobe mud off his boots. 'I knew it was you, Bill. Even before I rode out there and looked around, I felt it in my bones.' Ben raised his eyes to the other man. 'We spent a lot of time together. We talked a lot about robbing stagecoaches. Then I saw in an old newspaper where you had escaped.' Ben flung the stick away and sat watching the other man. Bill Ames had been Ben Castle's best friend in prison. They had shared many things, including the few laughs they'd had behind stone and steel. They had been close.

'Where was you?' Bill Ames asked again. 'In the damned ground? There wasn't a soul anywhere around. I made blessed certain of that. How did you—?'

'I wasn't out there, Bill . . . I guess it's just as well I wasn't. I just explained to you—I saw in a newspaper where you escaped. The rest of it . . . . hell, Bill, remember all those damned hot nights in summertime we'd lie awake sweating and talking?' Ben glanced over at the grazing horse, studied the shoulder-brand, which looked like an axe, and said, 'Whose outfit is that you ride for?'

'Tomahawk . . . They got a place for another man, Ben.'

'Naw . . . They're going to need *two* men . . . You got me in a bad spot, Bill. That driver you shot . . . he died and they buried him yesterday.'

'Did you know him?'

'Not exactly. I rode down here on his coach and we talked a little.' Ben glanced back in the direction of the darkly timbered mountainside, then turned back as he continued to speak. 'Yesterday the sheriff down at Kearneyville had a couple of federal marshals ride in. Then the sheriff went around lookin' for me. I lit out because sure as I'm sitting here those marshals knew me. Maybe Sheriff Shelby mentioned my name, I'm not sure what happened, but sure as hell those marshals knew me, knew what I was in prison for, and you can guess the rest. They and the sheriff would be fixing to set up an ambush and grab me.'

Bill Ames was listening with keen interest. 'Why would federal lawmen be down here? That wasn't no army payroll.'

'I don't know. I just know they're here, and if I'd hung around I'd have maybe got shot. At the least I'd have been jugged in the Kearneyville jailhouse while someone tried to make a case against me for robbing that stage, because that's what they did the other time I got into trouble with the law.'

Bill scowled. 'Tell you what, Ben. I think we had better both of us saddle up tonight and get

50

the hell out of this country. I don't like it anyway. I never liked working cattle.'

'How did you happen to come down here, Bill?'

'Kearneyville?' said the tawny-eyed man, and his lips pulled wide in a mirthless smile. 'I used to know a feller from down here. We worked together for a couple of years . . . He got away the day they ran me down after our last robbery together . . . He owed me. Ben, I needed a place to hide out for a little while, so I came lookin' for him. And you know what? The damned fool died a couple of years back.'

'Why didn't you head out?'

Ames shrugged. 'I was thinking about it when I run into the Tomahawk foreman in the saloon one afternoon and he offered me a riding job . . . Here I am . . . But now it's time to make a run for it. Deputy U.S. marshals are serious trouble. It sure is not like they was cowtown constables or sheriffs . . . Ben, I sure as hell had no idea you was within a thousand miles of this place, so help me.'

When Ames stopped speaking he raised his eyes to the gloomy mountainside behind Ben Castle, scanned among the tiers of big trees for a moment, then sighed and leaned to retrieve his sixgun.

Ben stopped him. 'Leave it be.'

Ames looked around faintly frowning.

Ben returned the hard stare. 'Like I told you,

Bill, if I'd let them get ahold of me, I'd have been unable to find you. You're going back to Kearneyville with me. You're going to tell that sheriff down there who got the pouch and shot the driver. That's the only way I can keep out of jail.'

Ames's thin-lipped wide mouth slowly pulled flat as he stared at his old friend. For a long time he gazed at Ben Castle without moving or speaking. Then he blew out a big, rough breath, shot another look behind Ben in the direction of the dark timber, and said, 'What difference does it make? You don't belong here anyway. Within three, four days we can be so far from here nobody will even know where this place is. Ben, one town is like another town.' Ames studied Castle's expression, and tried a different tack. 'They gave you twenty dollars and a suit of clothes when you got out. How much of that twenty you got left? Ben . . .' Bill Ames made an exaggerated glance all around, and leaned a little to speak again in a lowered tone. 'Sixty thousand dollars. Gawd. I never seen so much money before in my life—and neither have you . . . Out in San Francisco we could eat the best grub they got, set in poker games at tables with genuine red velvet on them and buy the fanciest clothes . . . Ben, I'll give you half . . . I got it hid . . . I was goin' to wait a little while, until the ruckus died down, then high-tail it . . . How about us leaving tonight?'

Castle gazed at his old friend throughout all this without speaking, without showing any expression, and when he finally spoke his voice had a dull hardness to it.

'Remember how we used to talk about the damned fools who shot folks for no reason, and how you agreed with everything I said, Bill? . . . You didn't agree with any of it, did you?'

'Ben, so help me that stage-driver was going for his sixgun.'

Ben spat aside, then leaned to arise, less angry than deeply disgusted. 'You're a liar. When they brought him to town the damned gun was in its holster with the tie-down in place . . . Get on your feet, Bill. It's a long ride from here to Kearneyville.'

CHAPTER SIX

THE CAPTIVE

Ames did not arise for a moment or two. He sat gazing up at Ben Castle. Eventually he reached for his hat, dropped it on and finally stood up. As they faced each other Ames's wide mouth pulled upwards very slightly, his tan eyes bored into Ben Castle, and he said, 'Remember what I used to tell you? You was too trustful with folks. That's how they caught up with you. You

53

always had some notion that once you rode away from a robbery, that was the end of it; folks wouldn't stay mad, they'd forget about it. Ben, you just wasn't cut out to be an outlaw.' As he finished speaking the faint smile broadened, the tan eyes got noticeably narrower. 'Turn around real slow, Ben.'

Castle did not move nor take his eyes off the other man's face. His stomach knotted.

From the same arroyo he had used to surprise Bill Ames, another man was standing in mud, visible from the waist up. He had a bull-neck, red hair, and pale eyes beneath the pulled-forward hatbrim which were fixed upon Ben Castle's back.

He cocked the sixgun in his right fist and spoke. 'Take his gun, Bill . . . Good; now then, mister, you sit down with your back to that tree, facing me, and keep both hands where I can see 'em.'

Ames made a bitter, derisive little laugh and pointed toward the tree where he had been leaning. 'I told you,' he said. 'If you got to be trustful, be damned awful careful about who you trust, and even then, don't trust 'em too much. Sit down.'

Ben sat and watched the red-headed man climb out of the arroyo. Up close, the stranger was more compact and muscular than he had looked from a distance. He had pale blue eyes and a sprinkling of freckles. He was not as old

54

as either Ben or Bill Ames, but he was close to being that old.

He kicked mud off as he watched Ames pick up his own weapon, holster it, then retrieve Ben Castle's sixgun. Bill gestured casually with a gunbarrel. 'This here is Herb Oliver the Tomahawk foreman. Herb, that there is my old friend from prison. His name is Ben Castle . . . How much did you hear while you was sneaking up?'

The Tomahawk foreman did not take his eyes off Ben when he answered. 'Enough. He was going to take you to town to the law . . . You did a pretty good job of keepin' him occupied. When did you see me in the gulch?'

'About fifteen minutes ago when I see that buckskin horse of yours sidle toward it from among them flaky little hills out yonder.' Bill also looked around, then he wagged his head. 'I'm not a praying man, but I darned near become one when I seen you get down into the gully.'

The rangeboss finally looked away from Ben Castle. 'His tracks were down there. He stalked you. Anyone else would have rode right on up.'

'Where's his horse?'

'Back yonder about a half mile. It's a livery animal from town.' Herb Oliver paused to glance at Ben again, then jerked his head for Bill Ames to walk out of hearing distance with him.

55

Ben watched them go. He could guess what they would discuss out of his hearing. The rest of it he had to piece together, but that did not prove to be difficult. If the Tomahawk foreman had not known about the robbery and shooting, he would not have come up behind them as he had to listen, before he threw down on Ben.

That could mean Herb Oliver had known about the robbery before Bill Ames had ridden down below town to commit it. But right or wrong, Oliver certainly knew about it now.

Ben tugged a grass stalk and chewed it while watching them out there. Bill had said he had not known the country, but he had robbed a stagecoach with a payroll-pouch on it. Maybe, as Sheriff Shelby had suggested, Bill had been lucky, but watching Ames and the rangeboss in conversation now, Ben thought it was more likely that someone had known that pouch would be on that particular stage the morning Ames shot Horseshoe Liston.

His guess was that the man who had known was Herb Oliver—unless there were others involved too.

When the conference was finished Oliver and Ames walked back with their eyes upon Ben Castle, but Bill Ames turned away before they reached the cottonwood trees, walking in the direction of the arroyo, while Herb Oliver stopped in front of Ben and stood gazing at him for a moment, before he hunkered down and said, 'Mister, this time you've stuck your head into the bear's mouth.'

Ben could have agreed, but instead he said nothing and studied the red-headed man. Oliver looked to be one of those individuals to whom breaking the law was a casual concern; he might do it often, or he might do it only very rarely, but when he did break the law, it was nothing he worried about. Ben wondered if he shot people in the back the same way, because as sure as hell, that was what he and Bill Ames had discussed out yonder.

Oliver removed a gnawed plug of chewing tobacco from a shirt pocket and bit off a corner, pocketed the plug, spat aside, and said, 'You was pretty shrewd to guess it was Bill who stopped that coach.'

Ben shrugged. 'When you spent as much time with someone as I spent with Bill, then come onto something like this, you just naturally figure he might have done it. And there was a little article in a newspaper about him escaping. But to tell you the truth right up until I recognised him sitting here in the shade this morning, I wouldn't have bet a plugged *centavo* I was right.'

'What difference did it make to you who did it?'

Ben considered his answer well before giving it. 'It wasn't the damned money. That driver was a nice feller. We talked a little on the way down here.' Ben paused, eyeing Herb Oliver, then decided to say no more. Nothing was going to influence Ames and Oliver, and Ben knew for a fact Bill Ames would sneer if Ben told them the real reason he had not wanted Horseshoe Liston's killer to go free. Looking at the pale-eyed, powerfully-muscled rangeboss in front of him, he decided Oliver would sneer too.

Herb Oliver spat again and looked back for some sign of Bill Ames. There was none so he faced Ben again, 'How much does Curtis Shelby know?'

Ben was slow again to offer an answer, but this time his reason was different. For as long as he could engage them in conversation, and if he could possibly plant even a very small fear in their minds, he was going to remain alive. *He* knew no one else had any idea who the highwayman had been, but neither of his captors knew this.

It was an almighty thin strand for a man to depend upon, unless he had no other.

He spoke slowly and quietly, hoping what he said would sound believable this way. 'Well, you see, Mister Oliver, I knew they'd try and blame that robbery and shooting on me because those two federal lawmen would know who I was and what I'd done to get sent to prison, but I didn't rob the coach nor shoot the driver. I went after the man who I figured could clear me, you see, and—'

'I didn't ask for a gawddamn sermon, just a simple answer to a question: How much does Curtis Shelby know?'

'Right now, I'd say he don't know very much beyond what he probably figures happened—me and someone else planning the robbery, me stayin' in town and the other feller committing it.'

Herb Oliver's irritable look vanished. He was about to arise when Ben spoke again.

'But you see, I had no idea what I might run into out here. Maybe even get shot. Maybe I wouldn't find Bill. So I wrote it all out exactly as I figured it happened, and sealed it in an envelope.'

Herb Oliver sank back to the ground staring at Ben. 'You named Bill Ames?'

'Yes,' lied Ben Castle unwaveringly returning the foreman's stare. 'An' I wrote that because I knew Bill very well, knew how he worked in the past, that sure as hell he did not figure all that out by himself—and he sure as hell wouldn't have known that particular coach had all that money on it.'

Oliver expectorated, studied the ground for a moment, then arose without another word and walked over to the edge of the arroyo. Bill did not come from down in there, he arrived atop the foreman's saddle animal leading Ben's livery horse, using a cow-trail which skirted southward of the arroyo. He saw Oliver looking for him and sang out.

Oliver immediately walked down to intercept Ames before he got within hearing of Ben Castle. They stood out there for a long time with the horses, their discussion sometimes heated, sometimes almost an intense whisper. When they turned toward the shade with Bill leading the horses, Ben heard the rangeboss say, 'It's not running. We got to do that anyway. It's havin' something back here with your name on it, and the fact that you worked for me on Tomahawk—and—the fact that we both ran for it at the same time. You understand?'

Bill's retort was a grumble. He glared at Ben when they walked on up. Six years of companionship ended at this exact moment. Ben read a death sentence in Ames's eyes.

Herb Oliver jettisoned his cud and planted powerful legs wide as he stared at Ben Castle. 'Who's got that envelope?' he demanded.

Ben's mind had been busy while his captors had been out with the horses. He had known this question would come so he was prepared to answer it. 'Nobody's got it. It's stuffed into a mattress at the roominghouse.'

Ames's murderous glare softened slightly. 'Herb, they might never find it in a damned roominghouse mattress. Who's going to look in—?'

'I told you, Bill, it's got to be burnt.'

Ames was exasperated and gestured with both arms. 'For Chris'sake, Herb, just the fact that we both leave tonight will give them plenty to go on. They won't need no damned letter.'

Oliver turned on his companion. 'We're not going to leave together tonight. We're going to get that damned envelope and burn it, then we're going to go on acting normal. I told you, Bill, I don't have no record as an outlaw and I'm not going to get one.'

Ames stared at the more compactly built man for a long time. Then in a lowered voice he spoke again. 'Herb, I already explained to you—if Castle don't turn up in town sure as hell they're going to start a manhunt.'

'Where we'll put Mister Castle no manhunter alive will find him,' stated the rangeboss. Then he said something which resolved a riddle which had been troubling Ben, who had been unable to understand just why, with all that money, the rangeboss was not willing to leave the country. Oliver said, 'My share is fine, Bill, but my share of Tomahawk ranch will make thirty thousand dollars of payroll money look like toothpicks. You understand? I talked a little about my plans when we was figuring out the stage robbery. Do you understand?'

When Ames stood scowling at the ground without speaking, Herb added a little more. 'All we need is that damned envelope. We'll put this

61

bastard where no one will ever find him. Ever. Then what have we got to worry about? Not a damned thing. We're both living good. We'll go right on living good up to the day I own Tomahawk, then we'll live like kings . . . Unless you want to take your half of the robbery money and start running. It's all right with me if you want to do that, Bill. I can find another partner for what I got to do at Tomahawk . . . You got any idea how much all those Tomahawk cattle and horses are worth, or how much the whole ranch will bring?' Oliver smiled at his companion. 'We'll go down yonder and find the damned envelope, burn it, then you can ride back with me, or you can head out and keep going.'

Oliver said no more, he went over to test two cinches and brought the saddled horses up into cottonwood shade. He looked down and said, 'On your feet, Castle.'

Ben arose and Ames watched him do it still with smouldering anger in the depths of his eyes. One thing Ben remembered very well about Ames was that if simple things became complicated he reacted with outbursts of temper.

The red-headed man did not order Ben to mount his horse, he stood looking at him for a long time then he said, 'Which room and which damned mattress?'

'The mattress of the bed I slept on last night.

I think the room was the third—or fourth—down the hall on the left-hand side.'

Oliver's brows dropped. 'You *think!*'

'It was dark when I rode in and got the room, and the damned lamp in the roominghouse hallway was so smoked up you couldn't see your hand in front of your face. I think it was the fourth room. Anyway, it was on the left-hand side of the hall.'

Herb glanced at Bill, whose face was darkening. 'He's making that bit up,' snarled Ames. 'He's stalling, Herb.'

Oliver did not dispute this. 'Maybe. Bill, neither you nor I can barge into that roominghouse and go into those rooms, especially the one this bastard has hired—but this son of a bitch can.' At Ames's loud groan the rangeboss shot back a fierce retort. 'Gawddammit, we already got sixty thousand at stake. What else we got at stake amounts to so much I can't even count that high.'

Bill was not listening. 'You want to take Ben down to Kearneyville, for Chris'sake?'

'Tonight. We'll get there after midnight. We'll go in with him. It'll take maybe fifteen minutes. That's not much time for what we're going to make, is it?'

Bill said, 'He's fooling you, Herb. I'll bet you a thousand dollars there ain't no envelope.'

Ben spoke for the first time since the argument had started. 'You'd lose the thousand dollars, Bill,' and Ames responded in a way Ben should have anticipated; with a roar he hurled himself forward, caught Ben before he got his feet untracked, and with one savage blow dumped Ben Castle unconscious on the ground.

Herb Oliver looked at the inert man, then up at Bill Ames. He did not say a word but his eyes glowed with an expression of speculative thought.

CHAPTER SEVEN

NIGHTFALL

When Ben recovered his jaw was swollen and his neck ached. He was lying in cool grass with Bill Ames sitting with his back against a saddle about thirty feet away. Bill's steady gaze was not particulary hostile, but it was lethal. Whatever had bound them together in the past no longer mattered. Bill tossed aside a grass stalk he had been chewing and said, 'Sit up. I didn't hit you that hard.'

Ben pushed around and sat up, did not look at Ames as he felt his puffy jaw, then rolled his head around very slowly to assess the extent of his sore neck. Evidently the impact of that unexpected blow had snapped his head backwards very hard.

When he finally glanced in Ames' direction the outlaw sneered. 'I always figured you for a fool, Ben. When Herb gets back we're goin' down to Kearneyville, and pardner I'll tell you for a fact that if there ain't any envelope, I'm going to walk you out into the middle of the road and leave your lousy body there for the town to find.'

Ben stopped moving his neck. The pain was a dull ache. Given a little time it would leave. He looked at Bill Ames. In all the years they had known each other he had never thought about Bill in terms of an enemy. Now, as he gazed at the outlaw, he could not consider him in any other way.

He sighed, felt his jaw again, moved it, then sank down upon one elbow. Dusk was close, which meant he had been knocked out for several hours.

Two saddleless horses were filling up on grass beyond the big old shaggy trees, and somewhere close by a resident toad was warming up with irregularly-spaced ugly croaks. The heat was leaving, although it had not been particularly bad this day, not as bad as it had been the previous few days.

Ben finally spoke. 'Bill, I think what you said about trusting folks is a two-way road.'

'What are you talking about?' the outlaw growled.

'Sixty thousand dollars . . . Why did Oliver

65

ride up into the mountains and leave you here at the spring?'

Ames's brow furrowed. His stare was about equal parts contempt and incomprehension. 'Because he wanted to get up high enough so's he could see all around. We didn't want those other riders comin' back.'

Ben thought about that, and looked northward. It was a very long ride just to view the countryside. Ames, seeing Ben's expression of scepticism, added a little more. 'I know what you're trying to do, but Herb Oliver and me been partners since before I come down here. You want to know something, Ben? Where you're going it won't make any difference. Herb's the one who paid a prison guard three hunnert dollars to leave a couple of doors unlocked so's I could get out. What do you think of that?'

Ben did not say what he thought of it, but that seemed to make no difference to Bill Ames, who arose and paced over where he could look eastward. Evidently he was getting impatient.

Ben watched him, and decided that Herb Oliver and Bill Ames had been friends a lot longer than Ben had thought. He also speculated that if Oliver paid to get Bill out of prison, it had been because Herb Oliver wanted to use Bill. The longer Ben thought about these things, the more grudging respect he began to have for Herb Oliver, who was clearly a man who made long-range plans, worked out each detail, then proceeded to do the things he planned. When Bill returned and sank down with a grunt, Ben had a question for him.

'That idea of taking over Tomahawk ranch didn't sound too reasonable to me, Bill.'

Evidently Ames had his own reservations, too, but all he said was: 'It don't have to sound reasonable to you. Herb's a real smart man. Personally, getting hold of a big ranch ain't something I'd care about. I like to make my money quick, and move on. But Herb will do it. Like I said, he's one smart son of a bitch.'

Ben looked at the dark-tinted evening sky. 'Smart enough to get the cache and head out in a dead run?'

Bill's temper flared. 'You think you can worry me? I know you pretty well, Ben, don't forget that. You can't get me all worried. I've known Herb more'n ten years. He ain't going to run off. Not with his other scheme in mind. Herb's one of them fellers like you and I'll never be—a real good thinker.'

Ben accepted all that, and worked his jaw. The soreness was diminishing but the swelling wasn't. Bill Ames grinned. 'You didn't know I could hit that hard, did you?'

Ben faced the grin. 'No. But then even a woman can hit hard when the other person's not expecting it. You're not a battler, Bill. I saw two fellers clean your plough in the prison yard,

67

remember?'

Ames sprang up and strode angrily away from the spring again, went out where the foothills would not interfere with distances, and squinted for sight of movement. He saw none, but less because there was none than because with night coming his visibility was limited. When he returned Ben had gone over to the spring to tank up on cold water. He walked back, ignored Bill's suspicious stare, and sank back down in the grass—with a fist-sized round granite rock under him. He held a wet handkerchief to his jaw, waited until Bill was seated, then said, 'If he don't get back soon, by the time we get down to Kearneyville two-thirds of the night will be gone.'

'What do you care?' snarled Ames, whose mood had been getting steadily worse the longer they had to sit there waiting. Then he said, 'That'd be like you. Write it down an' hide it in a damned mattress.' He sounded disgusted. 'You should have been a storekeeper.'

Ben smiled for the first time. 'As a matter of fact, I used to have some such notion in mind. Own a nice store in some pretty town where the people were friendly and they had shade trees and all.'

He slouched back, got his right hand curled around the granite rock, and watched Bill Ames yank his saddle around so he could rummage in the saddle bags. Bill brought forth some jerky wrapped in a greasy cloth. He concentrated on unwrapping the cloth very slowly in order to avoid leaving lint on the cured meat. Ben was also hungry, but the water had helped somewhat.

He shifted position a little. Bill did not look up. He was almost finished unwrapping the jerky.

Ben shifted a little more, sat up with one hand in his lap covering the other hand. 'You got enough jerky for two?' he asked.

Bill finally had the greasy rag unfolded. He ignored the question and leaned to examine the sticks of nearly black, pepper-cured shrivelled meat for lint.

Ben watched Ames closely, and raised his left hand as though to scratch. When Ames picked up a piece of jerky Ben brought up his right hand and also raised it shoulder high. The distance was no more than perhaps fifteen feet. His right hand moved without great speed; he wanted accuracy more than shocking-power. If the stone missed, before he could spring to his feet Bill Ames could draw and fire, and Ben had no illusions. Bill would kill him on the spot. He had never been impressed with that story of the hidden envelope. As Bill had said, he liked to make his money quickly, and run like hell afterwards.

The throw was direct, without great speed, and perfectly accurate. When the granite rock struck Ames barely in front of the ear, he did not even jerk upright in surprise, did not make any effort to turn or to flinch, he simply dropped the jerky, went forward and slightly sideways in the grass and did not make a sound.

Ben stood up, stepped over, flung away Ames's holstered sixgun, searched until he found his own weapon in one of the opened saddlebags, sank it into his holster, and finally returned to gag and tie the downed man.

Ames had straightened his legs and had flopped over onto his side. When Ben stopped above him and started to lean, Ames's left hand shot out, he grasped an ankle, and Ames flung himself backwards. Ben went down in a sitting position, astonished at what he considered an almost miraculous recovery from being stunned. He had not wasted more than a couple of minutes before approaching to tie his prisoner.

Ames rolled, got up onto all-fours, and sluggishly looked around as he heaved himself up off the ground. Ben was capable of faster movement and was back on his feet before Ames stood up. As they faced one another Ben could discern the signs of unsteadiness in his former friend. He made no move to use the gun in his holster. He said, 'Sit down.'

Ames started forward, shuffling over the grass as he brought up both arms and looked beyond them at his enemy. Ben shook his head.

He did not particularly want to do this, not to a man whose coordination and timing were badly off, but he did not want to be distracted either, if Oliver should appear.

Once more he spoke. 'You're out on your feet. Sit down, Bill.'

Ames made his lunge, which Castle avoided by simply stepping sideways, and when the outlaw's momentum carried him past, Ben moved in, rapped Ames on the right side, and when he came around Ben struck him a short, chopping strike over the heart followed by a higher, hard blow to the jaw.

Ames's knees turned loose, his hat fell off, he went down in the grass like a pole-axed steer, and this time when Ben bent over him to tug loose his shellbelt as well as his trouser belt, Ames was as inert as a sack of wet grain.

It required ten minutes to get the unconscious man trussed and gagged. Afterwards Ben returned to the spring to plunge both hands into cold water. He was still over there when he heard a horseshoe rattle pebbles somewhere south of the big trees out in the night.

Without wasting a moment he went back over, hoisted Ames's saddle and propped the unconscious man against it, yanked off the gag, dumped Ames's hat on his head, then resumed his earlier position nearby in a half-reclining position. His heart was beating so loud he could

71

hear it, or thought he could anyway.

The rider came steadily up out of the dusky night. When he was close he called ahead, but did not stop to await the response.

'Bill . . . ?'

Castle had never been a very successful mimic, the few times he had tried to be one, so he did not open his mouth. The oncoming horse continued to move ahead. When Ben could make out the recognisable, thick, compact silhouette, he eased out his sixgun but did not arise from the grass as he said, 'What the hell took you so long?' and made it sound like an angry, gruff snarl without attempting to make it also sound as though Ames had spoken.

Herb Oliver answered irritably as he walked his horse right on up. 'What do you mean; that's one hell of a long ride, and I couldn't leave the yard until Mrs Amy was in bed.' He was dismounting as he spoke. When he stepped to the head of his horse facing the propped up outlaw, Ben sat up, pointed the sixgun, and hauled back the hammer.

Oliver froze in surprise. Ben did not allow him the time to recover. He arose, stepped up, shoved the gunbarrel into Oliver's back, yanked the foreman's handgun out and hurled it backwards out into the night, then he moved away, coming around in a half circle until Herb Oliver could see him. The rangeboss's baffled gaze went from Castle to Ames, and back again to Ben Castle. The semi-darkness had done for Ben what he had hoped very hard it would do; it had obscured the fact that the man leaning against his saddle was unconscious.

Herb Oliver let go with a big gust of expelled breath. Astonishment rarely lasted very long with him. He was eyeing Castle at the same time he was already beginning to make the changes required by a totally new situation. He said, 'Put up the gun. You don't need it.' Then he relaxed a little and shook his head. 'After all that damned fool's been through no one should be able to get the drop on him.'

Ben motioned with his handgun. 'Sit down with both hands on your legs. *Sit!*'

Oliver obeyed as though he had wanted to sit down. With his head slightly to one side he studied his captor. 'You're pretty handy,' he said in a neutral, almost admiring tone of voice.

Ben hunkered twenty feet in front. 'Where is the sixty thousand dollars?' he asked.

Oliver raised and lowered powerful shoulders.

'You got to find that out from Bill. It's his loot.'

For a moment they looked at each other, then Ben repeated the question, but this time with his gunhand raised enough so that the rangeboss could see the trigger-finger tightening noticeably inside the trigger-guard. 'You got a minute,' Ben told the muscular, red-headed man. 'That's all.'

Herb Oliver was capable of swift thought, judgments and decision, but even if he had not been, a cocked sixgun about twenty feet away in the hand of a man who looked as though pulling the trigger would not trouble him, would have brought some kind of response even from an idiot. 'It's in the blacksmith shop at the ranch. We hid the pouch at the bottom of a sack of coal.'

'Who is Mrs Amy?'

Oliver had not expected that. 'Well . . . she's the widow of old Walt Edmond. He died four years back and she took over running the ranch.'

'She owns Tomahawk?'

Oliver nodded slightly, and Ben thought back to that compact, brisk-walking individual he had watched go from the main-house to the bunkhouse during his vigil atop the landswell before full daylight had arrived that morning.

Ames groaned and let his head flop to one side as consciousness began to return. Herb looked at him but Ben Castle did not take his eyes off the rangeboss. Bill Ames was a killer, a thief, and a few other things, but he was not clever and he was not devious. Herb Oliver was both and as Ben sat there reaching a decision he told Oliver to lift his pantslegs. There was a flat-handled bootknife-scabbard sewn into the outside top of his right boot. Ben shook his head. 'Get rid of that thing,' he growled. Then he ordered the foreman to lie face down in the grass.

He belted both arms behind the rangeboss's back, yanked him to his feet and told him not to move. Getting Ames to his feet was a little more difficult because after being stunned twice over a short period of time, the outlaw was unsteady and disoriented.

It required time for Ben to bring in two horses, saddle them, boost both his prisoners into their saddles, drape their lariats around their necks, then take both sets of reins and start walking as he led the two burdened saddle animals back down where he had left his horse.

CHAPTER EIGHT

AN ELEGANT COLT PISTOL

The night was deathly silent as the little cavalcade rode eastward. The men with hands belted in back were impassive until it began to dawn on the rangeboss that they were not riding toward Kearneyville, then he said, 'Where are you going, Castle?'

The reply shocked both captives into a long silence. 'Over to Tomahawk ranch.'

When the surprise passed Herb Oliver said, 'Why?'

'Because as late as it is now, by the time we got down to Kearneyville it'd be past dawn and me being a wanted man—riding in with you two as prisoners most likely wouldn't sit too well. Especially after you two respectable local citizens spun out enough lies to maybe get me hung.'

Bill Ames scowled at the rangeboss, but Oliver did not notice that as he said, 'Going to the ranch headquarters isn't going to help you, either.'

For a quarter of a mile Ben said nothing, and when he finally spoke it was in a voice as dry as corn husks. 'Maybe not, rangeboss. I've been hungry all day and I'm still hungry. I'll get something to eat down there.'

As Oliver and Ames exchanged a dark and baffled look, their captor went on speaking.

'And I want that money pouch at the bottom of the coal sack. I also want Mrs Edmond to hear what you two have been planning, and I think if someone from the ranch lopes down to town and fetches back Sheriff Shelby and those two federal lawman, I'll stand a better chance of getting my story told first.'

When he finished speaking Ben rubbed his scratchy jaw, felt the swelling and gazed at his prisoners. They looked away without making a sound.

The moon had finally arisen, but its meagre

light added little to the starshine, so the land they passed over was not only quiet, it was also too sooty for visibility to be very good.

Ben rolled and lit a smoke. It did not do as much toward alleviating his hunger pangs as cold water had done back at the cottonwood spring.

They were more than half way toward their destination when the rangeboss abruptly said, 'Castle, a smart man would slip in the yard in the darkness, up-end that coal barrel, get the money-bag, and hightail it.'

Ben nodded about that. 'The trouble is, I'm not a smart man.'

Ames grunted a retort to that. 'And you never was.'

Oliver ignored the interruption. 'She'll never believe you, Castle. I been her rangeboss for a long time. I was her husband's tophand. You're a stranger, a damned parole convict. You'll be lucky if she don't ring the triangle on the front porch and get everyone after your hide with rifles.'

Ben smoked, said nothing, and tried to see rooftops. He had already considered the very thing Herb Oliver had just brought up. He thought he probably had a good answer to it, but he did not mention it, and after he smashed out the cigarette atop the saddlehorn, he yawned and ignored the men riding loosely on his right side.

He was bone-tired. Not just from postponing some meals, but also because he had taken a lot of physical abuse today, and it had been a very long one, the kind of day a man did not expect to encounter more than a few times during his lifetime.

He detected a weak scent of woodstove smoke long before they were close enough to be able to skyline rooftops. Wood smoke reminded him of ovens and food.

Finally, with the buildings discernible as great, lumpy dark squares, he led the way northward until, where they would enter the yard, the big log barn would block a view, if anyone was watching, which Ben did not think very likely at this time of night. Oliver and Ames were grim and silent as they came around toward the upper end of the yard.

Ben halted, swung his leg over the horn, slid to the ground and turned. 'Not a sound. Get down.'

He did not explain how this was to be accomplished with their hands tied in back, he simply stood there waiting.

It was not as difficult as it seemed, providng the prisoners dismounted as Ben had done, which they both did.

He gestured for them to walk ahead of him while he led the horses to the barn. He did not enter. It was abysmally dark in there. He looped reins, tugged latigos loose, dumped saddles in the dirt, motioned for Oliver and Ames to walk ahead in the direction of the corrals, and took the animals back there to be turned in.

Afterward, he stood gazing at his prisoners. They stared back. Ben said, 'If you're thinking about hollering, forget it. I'll split your skulls with a pistol barrel . . . Walk along the rear of the buildings to the back of the main-house . . . Not a damned sound.'

Herb Oliver looked disbelieving. 'The main-house . . . ? That three-sided shed across the yard is where the coal barrel is.'

Ben pointed. 'Toward the main-house, and not a damned sound.' As he lowered his arm he continued to regard the rangeboss. 'I'm looking for a chance, boss-man. Even a little one will be enough . . . *Walk!*'

They walked. In the stillness every footfall made some noise. Ben swore to himself but as careful as he tried to be, his own footfalls made sound.

But they reached the west side of the main-house, where he halted them, gun in hand, and asked if Mrs Edmonds always locked her doors at night. Herb Oliver did not know whether she did or not, at least that was what he said. When Ben asked where the rear door was, Oliver jerked his head toward the far corner of the building. 'Around yonder.'

'Where is her bedroom?'

'Next to the back door.'

Ben sighed and turned them back toward the front of the house. To succeed at what he had in mind, he had to possess the initiative. He could not risk being met inside the house by a grim old female rancher with a rifle in her hands.

At the porch he halted them long enough for him to make certain no one had seen them, or was at least out in the yard, then he flagged them ahead with his gunbarrel and offered some good, half-whispered advice.

'Keep to the left on the steps and on the porch. Don't step out where the boards will squeak.'

Oliver looked around. 'Sure. But that won't get you inside.'

Ben pointed the gun and Oliver led off, staying to the side of the boards where they had been nailed into solid underpinning. Perhaps it had been an unnecessary precaution because even when Ben stepped over to try the door, the boards did not yield under his weight.

The door was loose to his push, but was barred from inside. Now, he wished had had not made the foreman throw away that narrow-bladed bootknife. There was a crack between the moulding and the door wide enough to slip a narrow blade through, get it beneath the bar, and lift the bar carefully out of its hangers.

He motioned for his prisoners to stay ahead,

and moved to a large window to the east of the barred door. It too was barred from within. He motioned for the captives to keep moving around the house from window to window. Where he finally was rewarded it was not a window, it was a narrow side-door on the east side of the house which opened from a very large kitchen to the shaded expanse of porch on that side of the house. It was probably used on laundry days when wet-wash would be draped to dry from a pair of old lariats stretched between the wall and a porch upright.

Now, with a way into the house, Ben leathered his weapon, grabbed the britches-waistbands of his two prisoners and, guiding them this way, went through the kitchen into a large parlour where starshine made a faint, ghostly light. There were several big, oval-framed pictures over a large stone mantle where the blackened fireplace stood. There was quite a bit of other furniture, which Ben looked at only because he did not want to stumble over any of it as he hauled back on Herb Oliver and whispered.

'Which way?'

Oliver could have asked the obvious question, but he didn't, he jutted his jaw Indian-fashion toward an open doorway leading into a very dark hallway. Ben gave him a slight shove, then did the same to Bill Ames.

There were dimly visible closed doors along

the corridor. Only one door was open. The room beyond was very large which was fortunate because the huge old bedstead, dresser, chifferobe and chairs, were massively heavy furnishings.

Ben eyed the bed with its centred large lump, pushed his prisoners inside the room, then pointed to chairs upon the opposite side of the room, and waited until Ames and Oliver were seated, watching him like eagles, their lips flattened in bleak silence.

He moved to the bedside and studied the sleeping woman. About all that was visible was a mass of light hair and one hand pushed upwards from beneath the blankets.

He raised the lamp mantle, struck a match, set it to the wick, lowered the mantle and waited for the light to brighten while he watched the woman.

She did not awaken. He glanced at his prisoners. They could have been made of stone. He leaned to gently shake the sleeping woman's shoulder. She still did not awaken. He shook harder, had to do that three times, and when she finally opened her eyes and saw an unshaven, sunken-eyed, evil-appearing stranger leaning over the bed, she did not cry out, and she only moved slightly by shoving her exposed hand quickly beneath the pillow as her dark violet eyes widened to their limit and did not leave Ben's face.

He reached across and pinned the moving wrist. Then he groped beneath the pillow with his other hand, found the weapon and pulled it out into the light. It was a double-action Lightning Colt, nickel plated, with mother-of-pearl grips, and two golden overlayed initials on the barrel: A.E.

Ben put the gun aside and said, 'Just listen, Mrs Edmond.'

She started to sit up, finally, pulling blankets with her. Ben eyed her quizzically, then glanced over at Herb Oliver. 'Is this the owner?'

Oliver noded and started to say something, but Ben cut him off. 'Shut up. Not a damned word.'

He looked at the woman again. He had expected a much older woman, with the leathery skin which went with ranch women who had worked beside their husbands. This woman was no more than perhaps thirty-five or thirty-eight. She was neither grey nor leathery. She was, in fact, very handsome, even after being awakened from a sound sleep.

Ben met her gaze and started to talk. He did not stop for fifteen minutes. Amy Edmond did not interrupt. In fact she scarcely looked away. Only once did she glance at her foreman and Bill Ames. That was when Ben told her what Ames had told him while Oliver was back here at the ranch. Even when Ben told her what he had heard Oliver arguing about with Ames,

83

comparing what the ranch would be worth to them compared with the payroll loot, she did not take her eyes off Ben.

When he finished, she said. 'Sit down,' and inclined her head toward a chair.

Ben sat. He watched her turn toward Herb Oliver when she spoke in the same crisp, no-nonsense tone of voice as she had used in ordering Ben to be seated.

What she said surprised Ben. 'He was lying, wasn't he, Herb?' Then, as Oliver came to life for the first time in several hours, she held up a hand to prevent him from speaking. 'You'll have plenty to say. You always have had, Herb.' She lowered the hand. 'Get down on your knees and look under the bed.'

Oliver blinked at her.

'Do as I said, Herb. Look under there.'

He left the chair, glanced at Ben and Bill Ames as though he considered this ridiculous, then ducked down, looked, stayed crouched a long time, and eventually pulled back and stood up, would not meet anyone's eyes, and got back into the chair, finally meeting the dark violet eyes of the handsome woman.

She said, 'Tell Bill and this man, Herb.'

But Oliver did not speak. He glanced from Ben to Bill, then leaned back and let go a long, audible sigh. She was unrelenting. 'They're waiting. *What is under there?*'

Instead of answering, the rangeboss put a

long gaze upon Amy Edmond and asked a question. 'How did you find it?'

Her answer was flat-toned and unembellished. 'Tony and Stub had that big chestnut colt over there to put shoes on. They didn't cross-tie him. He started kicking and broke the coal barrel . . . Stub came up here to the house looking as though he had met a ghost . . . It was Bill Ames, wasn't it, Herb?'

Oliver remained silent, and Ben, who was watching him, saw colour draining from the foreman's face. He almost felt sorry for Oliver.

The handsome woman faced Ben. 'What did you say your name was?'

'Ben Castle, and before anyone says anything else, I was in prison for six years for stage-robbery. That's where I met Bill Ames . . . Just so you will know.'

The violet eyes lingered upon Ben. 'You said you thought you knew who robbed that coach.'

'Yes'm.'

'As a stage-robber, Mister Castle, why did you feel impelled to hunt Bill down?'

'In the first place, ma'm, I'm not a stage-robber. I *was* a stage-robber. In the second place, there was no call to shoot the driver. Bill told me the driver tried to draw on him. That's a lie. When they brought Mister Liston to town his sixgun was still in its holster with the tie-down still knotted . . . I don't like cold-blooded killers. Also, Mister Liston did me a favour

85

which don't have anything to do with the rest of this. I owed him for that.'

She was prepared to speak again when Ben stood up and shook his head to silence her. 'Lady, another time I'll answer questions. Right now if you'll send someone to Kearneyville for the sheriff, I'll go raid your cookhouse, then I'm going to bed down in the hay for fifteen hours, and after that I'm going to eat again, hunt up a creek for a bath . . . then we can talk if you're still of a mind to.'

He picked up her elegant little gun and handed it to her. 'Shoot 'em if you want to. It's fine with me.' He went to the door and turned to also say, 'I'll roust up your riders and send them over here.' His gaze drifted to Ames and Oliver who were watching him. He met their stares for a moment, then turned on his heel and walked away without saying another word.

CHAPTER NINE

TOMAHAWK

There were three men at the bunkhouse and when Ben kicked open the door, lighted the lamp, then roughly shook each of them awake, they stared and rubbed their eyes.

'Miz Edmond's got Ames and Oliver in her

room over at the main-house. She needs you fellers to lend her a hand keepin' an eye on them. Get up.'

Only one man obeyed, the other two stared, then began to look hostile. Ben smiled at them. 'She'll tell you the story. Take your handguns.' He met the steady looks for a moment then also said, 'My name is Ben Castle. She can tell you about me too . . . Gents, go lend her a hand.'

He stepped to the door and looked back. All three men were reaching for their britches and boots.

He trudged to the cookhouse, which was dark, lighted a table lamp and was rummaging in the floor-cooler when a large, awry-haired older man wearing floppy slippers entered the big room from out back stuffing shirt-tails into his britches and looking indignant. He did not recognise Ben Castle so he stopped in the doorway, finished with the shirt-tail while studying the intruder, and finally said, 'Who the hell are you? What are you doing in here?'

Ben took a platter of cold roast beef to the long table, went back for some buttermilk in a crockery pitcher, then smiled at the angry *cocinero* as he sat down to eat, using his clasp-knife as a utensil. 'Name is Ben Castle. I just came from Mrs Edmond.' He paused at slicing cold meat because that had not sounded right. 'Oliver and Ames are over there. She's keepin' a gun on them. Mister, it's a long story.' Ben started to eat without saying another word, not even when the older man irritably slammed kindling into his stove and noisily rattled a big coffeepot, then turned with a scowl and said, 'What the hell are you talking about?'

Ben went on eating. His hunger was a cumulative thing; once he began eating the hunger seemed to increase rather than decrease. The buttermilk was cold and fresh. It also signified that Tomahawk ranch kept a cow, which most cattle outfits did not do because rangemen looked on cow-milking as demeaning. It also signified that someone, probably the big old disgruntled cook, made butter.

The fire snapped, heat came slowly into the room, and when the aroma of coffee spread, the cook came over to lean on the table with a menacing look as he said, 'What's going on? Why would Miz Edmond hold a gun on the foreman?'

Ben looked up with his mouth full and his jaws working. When he could speak, he simply said, 'Go on over to the main-house and see for yourself.'

He and the cook exchanged a long look before the older man straightened back off the table. He did not leave the cookhouse, he instead drew off a cup of hot coffee and brought it to the table with him, sat down with a loud groan, and sat hunched like a resting bear, solemnly watching Ben demolish that big chunk of left-over roast beef he had intended to make hash out of.

Ben finished eating, finished emptying the pitcher of buttermilk, and feeling more human and less tired now, he smiled. 'I'm obliged, partner. Is there a hay loft to that log barn?'

The cook nodded.

Ben arose. 'I been a long time without sleep. I'll be up there in the hay—if Mrs Edmond wants me—for the rest of you, the first one who pokes his head up through the crawl-hole, I'll blow it off.' He returned the big, older man's gaze for a moment in silence, then started for the door. He was in the opening when the *cocinero* called after him.

'Are you a lawman?'

The answer was short. 'No.'

Ben was crossing the yard with a very faint brightness beginning to show and saw a lean youth come out of the main-house hastening in the direction of the cookshack. Ben reached the front barn-opening before the hurrying rider saw him and called over.

'I'm goin' to town for Shelby . . . This is the damndest thing I ever heard of.'

Ben watched the cowboy enter the cookhouse, and thought to himself that regardless of the rider's breathlessness, he still had not forgotten that it was a long ride down to Kearneyville, on an empty stomach.

The barn was very large and had that pleasant smell most old barns had. It was also dark. Ben groped his way until he located the loft ladder, and started climbing.

There was timothy hay up there, freshly cured and crinkly underfoot. As a youngster he had thought there could be no more pleasant fragrance than the kind cured hay made. Years later when he had smelled perfume, he had still thought hay-scent was sweetest.

He kicked off his boots, shed his hat, put his coiled shellbelt under his right hand, and sank back into the hay. Whatever Mrs Edmond did, whatever Sheriff Shelby did, whatever anyone else in the whole damned world did, they were going to do it without Ben Castle. He was asleep within moments.

Morning arrived, sunlight brightened a fresh new day, a man down below brought in the horses Ben and his companions had ridden to cuff and clean and put in stalls which had hay in the mangers. The cook had relayed what Ben had said about being disturbed to Mrs Edmond and she had passed orders no one was to climb up to the hay loft.

Heat built up beneath the barn roof. By mid-afternoon it was much hotter in the loft than it was down below, or even outside the yard.

When Ben finally awakened he was sweating. There was a loft door in the front wall, but it was closed, which was customary because no

90

one wanted wild pigeons roosting and nesting in their hay lofts; they ruined a lot of hay, so the little loft doors were kept closed.

He was comfortable. Too warm but neither thirsty nor hungry, and willing to suffer from a little heat just to be able to lie there without moving or having to listen to conversation, or even to do much thinking, but inevitably the thoughts arrived.

He viewed them all with something close to fatalistic indifference, and finally sat up, knocked off hay and reached for his boots. He wanted to find a creek and soak his carcass in it.

When he came down the loft ladder the barn was empty and the yard was quiet. There were three horses eating in stalls which he recognised. One of them was his livery animal. Upon the opposite side of the barn there were another three horses in stalls, but they were simply dozing.

He went out back. There was no one back there either. Southward about a half-mile there was an uneven line of water-willows which curved and bent on a course which was roughly from the northeast to the southwest. Water willows grew alongside creeks and no place else. He re-set his old hat and started walking.

Once, while he was passing behind the bunkhouse, he heard someone talking, but the words were indistinguishable, and he did not care what was being discussed anyway. Again,

91

as he passed the main-house on the west, shady side, he heard voices. This time he thought one of them belonged to a woman. He kept on walking toward the creek.

There were some loafing crows among the creek-willows. When Ben pushed through to find the creek they flung upwards in ungainly flaps, screaming imprecations at the two-legged intruder for startling them, and went northward in an untidy flight, still making raucous sounds.

There was a widened place where someone years back had created a rock dam so the water would spread. It was not very deep. A steel mirror was hanging from a willow limb and there was another indication that this bathing-hole was still used: On a cracked board nailed to a willow tree was a straight-razor and the remains of a bar of brown lye-soap.

Ben shed off, gasped at the chill of the water, got nicely settled with his head resting on a round boulder, and let the coursing water do the rest. He eventually used the soap, then got back down flat out to soak some more.

There were some puffy white clouds in the sky, the heat came straight down, and he watched a soaring red-tailed hawk make its increasingly wide sweeps, moving farther away with each circle until Ben could no longer see it.

He thought those three unfamiliar horses in the barn might belong to Curtis Shelby and the pair of federal lawmen. If so, then they were at the main-house with Mrs Edmond.

He sat up, leaned forward to wash his hair and thought about Bill Ames. Friendship was a fragile thing. He felt saddened by the destruction of it, but that was all he felt about Ames.

He thought of Herb Oliver while flinging his head back for his hair to dry. A small, dainty yellow and black striped snake no longer than the distance between a man's wrist and elbow came through the grass to reach cool creek-mud, and Ben made a philosophical observation to him which the snake ignored because he was thirsty and nothing else mattered to him.

'This world is full of horses' asses. More horses' asses in fact than there are horses. There are smart ones and dumb ones. Bill Ames is a dumb one. Oliver is a smart one. The dumb ones trip themselves up soon. The smart ones need a little more time, but they get tripped up too . . . Snake, I got a hunch that if you can stay in tall grass where hawks can't find you, you're going to live a lot longer than Bill Ames . . . Oliver, I don't know. But one of these days . . .'

The snake was departing, Ben's hair was almost dry, and he felt more refreshed than he had felt in days. The sun was slightly off centre on its way westward. Its heat would dry Ben off in minutes.

He waded out of the water, made certain there were no biting ants or other unfriendly critters on a flat rock, then sat on it for the sun to dry him.

It was a good time for reflection. His wish to find a place where his past would never overtake him had failed. He felt slightly regretful about that because he had truly liked the Kearneyville country and most of the people he had met in it.

He was forty years old and had wasted the last half-dozen or so of those years. What he needed was . . .

Two dry twigs snapped in quick succession somewhere behind him out through the willow screen. He arose and stepped over to the pile of clothing, picked up his Colt and turned, waiting for the next sound of someone sneaking up through the willows.

There was silence.

He crouched trying to peer through the dense undergrowth. What he sought was movement. When it finally appeared as a pale blur Ben swung the gun toward it, scarcely breathing.

A throaty voice said, 'Mister Castle?'

He froze. It was a woman's voice. The only woman was the lady from the ranch. He dropped the gun and reached desperately for his britches.

'Mister Castle? It's Amy Edmond. One of the men said he thought he saw you come over here

. . . Mister Castle, are you decent?'

Ben was struggling with the trousers when he answered her. 'No, ma'm, and I'd as soon you went away, if you don't mind.'

She said, 'I'll wait.'

He did not reply. When he had his trousers on and reached for his boots, a scorpion crawled out of one boot. He flicked it away and beat both boots to dislodge anything else which might have crawled in.

'Mister Castle? Curtis Shelby took Ames and my foreman back to town with him.'

Ben was pulling on a boot when he politely said, 'That's nice, ma'm.'

'Are you dressed yet?'

'No ma'm.'

'It takes you longer to get dressed than it does a woman.'

He pulled at the second boot without answering that remark. Then he stood up, stamped, and picked up his soiled, sweat-stiff old faded shirt. If he'd had anything else at all, even a blanket, he would not have put the shirt on, but he had nothing else.

Finally, with his gunbelt buckled carelessly into place, he dropped the old hat on his head and leaned to part the willow limbs. She was in speckled shade about a hundred feet southward, down near the dammed-up place. Maybe it was the shade, but she did not look more than about eighteen. But she was solidly, compactly put

95

together, and that did not ordinarily go with being eighteen. At least that was his thought as he leaned peering out at her.

She was very pretty. He wagged his head. He had meant to borrow that old straight-razor before returning to the yard. His beard never grew straight. It curled as though he had ring-worm. It was also several different colours, reddish, brownish, and lately, also a little greyish.

He wondered if she would return to the yard if he asked her to, and decided that she would not, pushed the willows aside and ploughed through out into the shaded sunlight where she watched him emerge with those very dark, violet-blue eyes studying him.

He smiled, conscious of the disreputable picture he made with his hair too long, his beard a shambles, and his clothing faded, soiled, and dirty.

She said, 'It was a long session, Mister Castle . . . Herb . . . I remember my father saying people only think they know other people, they never really do. This is the first time I ever thought he was right. Herb was so different from the man I've known for so long.'

She strolled a little closer in the shade, and looked over in the direction of the yard. When she looked back again, she smiled slightly. 'Curtis Shelby . . . when I told him why you went after Ames, he said that was the best thing he's heard about you in the last couple of days.'

Ben had a question for her. 'What about those federal marshals; they came out with him didn't they?'

'Yes. Did you think they were looking for you?'

'Well, no, not exactly. But I didn't want to run into them.'

'Why? You served your sentence and were honourably released.'

He rubbed his stubbled jaw and eyed her a trifle sceptically. There was no point in discussing something like this, which she probably would not understand anyway, so he said, 'I guess I'll saddle up and head on out.'

'To Kearneyville?'

'No. Just head out.'

'Curtis wants to talk to you, Mister Castle.'

He nodded at her. 'There is nothing more to talk about. Did they take the payroll pouch back with them?'

'Yes.'

'And they got Ames for killing Mister Liston. They got his partner, Herb Oliver. From here on it's up to a law court.'

She was studying him again, her very dark blue eyes unwavering. 'Are you ready to walk back? By now you're probably hungry again.'

That was true enough. He was indeed hungry again. He put his head slightly to one side as he gazed at her and said, 'I got a hunch about you,

97

Mrs. Edmond. I think you're one of those folks who've got iron up their backs who talk real easy, always seem to agree, and in the end get their own way.'

She suddenly laughed. He thought for a damned fact she really did look eighteen, and she was as pretty as a speckled bird.

'Mister Castle, what do you think I want?'

'For me to go down yonder and talk to Sheriff Shelby.'

She still had the twinkle in her eyes when she replied. 'You're right. But I want to ride down with you.'

He batted at a deer-fly. 'Why?'

She turned toward the distant yard. 'After you've been fed we can sit on the porch and talk.' She looked at him, and smiled again.

He sighed and started walking beside her.

CHAPTER TEN

SOMETHING UNEXPECTED

She did not lead him to the cookhouse, where her riders were eating in solemn silence because the events of this particular day had shaken them up badly, she took him to the main-house, handed him a razor, told him where the wash-house was, then she went to her kitchen to

98

prepare a meal.

The razor was honed sharp, which was a blessing. Ben had never enjoyed shaving his particular beard with dull razors. When he had finished and opened the wash-house door, there were some clean clothes lying across an old sawhorse, and someone had placed the sawhorse so that if he didn't see the clothing, he would fall over the thing.

He looked up in the direction of the house. The last person who had signified their distaste over his soiled appearance by laying out clean clothes for him had been his mother. And that had been a very long time ago.

He re-dressed. For a fact he felt much better in something clean. The shirt was about right, the trousers were a mite short but otherwise fitted well enough. He stood in the fading daylight thinking about the man who had undoubtedly owned those clothes. He remembered being told that her husband had died four years ago. Or was it five?

His face stung but at least it felt cleaner as he went over to the back door and rapped once, then entered. The big old house smelled of cooking meat and something he thought might be frying spuds with onions mixed in.

He went through to the kitchen doorway. She did not see him. He watched her work. She was muscular, did everything with easy confidence, and when she finally turned and saw him she

99

blushed.

He had to say something so he said, 'It'll take a while to get that razor sharp again. I'm much obliged for the use of it.'

She picked up a water glass and handed it to him without a word. Then she went back to the stove. He held the glass, wondering if he had said something to upset her. But she looked arond and said, 'You don't look like the same man, Mister Castle. Soapy can cut your hair, if you'd like. Soapy is the *cocinero* . . . I hope you like pan-roasted steak.'

He tasted the whiskied water. He liked just about everything people cooked to eat, and right now he could probably have eaten the tail off a snake if someone was holding its head.

'I'll like anything you cook,' he said, without meaning to be gallant, so he was surprised when she turned, blushing again, and smiled directly into his eyes.

A rider came to the front porch and rapped. Amy Edmond handed Ben the big fork for turning the meat and went across the parlour to the doorway. She returned moments later to say, 'There is a straggle of Indians passing to the west.' At his expression of enquiry she explained. 'Every year they pass by heading for the mountain meadows to hunt and cure meat for winter. Every year I send one of the men out with sugar and coffee . . . He'll be back in a few minutes ready to ride.' She smiled and pointed

100

to a chair at the table. Ben obediently sat down with his branch-water and whisky.

'My father started that about the time I was born. He used to say it's cheaper to donate to them now and then than it was to fight them. Only now, there is no fight left in them.'

He was less interested in the Indians than he was in something else she had said. 'Your father started Tomahawk ranch?'

'Yes. Eight years before I was born. He and my mother are buried . . . I'll show you, tomorrow.' As she said this she went to a large cupboard for sacks of sugar and coffee, which she took to the front porch and left there. When she returned she put food on the table and sat opposite Ben, looking at him.

'Can we be friends?' she asked.

He blinked in surprise.

'What I mean is—as a friend can I ask why you robbed a stage, Mister Castle?'

He reddened and considered the platter of food. 'Because I was a fool. Young, back then, out of work, and a fool to boot . . . I got twenty-seven dollars and they overtook me the very next day as I was down in a gully watering my horse . . . Got caught like a ten-year-old kid.'

She continued to watch him for a moment or two, then reached for her knife and fork. 'It's been a long time since I've cooked a meal for anyone,' she said.

101

He followed her example and picked up the utensils to eat with. 'I don't even have to taste it to tell that you're a fine cook, Mrs Edmond.'

'Is that so?'

'Sure,' he said, wrinkling his nose, and she laughed.

Now an awkward silence settled between them. Ben ate without worrying much about that. He was not especially knowledgeable about females, but he knew people. Even among old friends these interludes of awkwardness arrived.

He glanced over at her a couple of times. She was eating without a lot of enthusiasm, as though having him here in her kitchen at supper with her might have stirred some memories.

When he had finished and was reaching for the whisky glass, her eyes lifted to his as he said, 'I'll tell you a little story, if you'd care to listen.'

She nodded, and he told her why he had come to the Kearneyville country, and also why he would now have to leave it. He told her those things because he wanted to jar her away from unpleasant memories. He must have succeeded because when he finished speaking and drained his glass, she spoke briskly to him.

'That is no reason to leave, Mister Castle. No matter where you go, the past will go with you. I'd say over a period of years it will also come up and confront you. Maybe not exactly as it has here, but in some way it will.'

He was comfortable, rested, fed, and warmed by the whisky, so he leaned back gazing straight over at her. She was not like a girl, although at times she looked like one. He thought that operating Tomahawk ranch by herself had probably pulled up a toughness in her she might never otherwise have shown. She was smart—for a female.

She returned his gaze. 'I need a rangeboss, Mister Castle.'

That jarred him. Until last night she had never seen him. Until this afternoon they had never spoken at any length together. 'For all you know I beat horses, shoot people, hate little kids and dogs.'

Her humour showed gently. 'I don't own a dog, there are no children on the ranch, and you neither beat horses nor shoot people.'

'How do you know I don't?'

'Because I looked that livery horse over while you were at the creek. He's been cared for. Probably better than his owner in Kearneyville cares for him. And if you shot people—why didn't you shoot Bill Ames when you fought him?'

'How did you know about that?'

'He told me . . . Would you like me to mix you another whisky and water?'

'No ma'm. I'm not much of a drinker. But

that tasted fine.'

'Would you care to go out on the porch? It's a beautiful evening.' As she said this she arose.

He also stood up. 'I'll help clean up the dishes,' he told her, and saw the laughter in her eyes. 'It won't be the first time, ma'm . . . When I was a little kid my mother used to say that was the only times I really got my hands clean.'

She shook her head and led the way out to the porch. She had been correct, it was indeed a beautiful evening, and from the slightly raised main-house porch the view of the yard, all the outbuildings, and even the far-distant mountains, was something to bring peace to a man's heart. Maybe to a woman's heart as well.

They sat in late evening shadows with the very faint fragrance of all the countryside coming up to them. He remembered his makings and would have rolled a smoke, but they were in the shirt he had left on that sawhorse out back, so he stretched his legs instead, and turned to gaze at her profile.

Without looking around she said, 'This has been a terrible day for me.'

He understood that.

'I depended on Herb so much, Mister Castle.'

He could understand that too, and it prompted him to make a statement about her offer at supper. 'I've never been a rangeboss.

Just a rider. Not even a strawboss.'

She turned, finally, to look at him. 'Did you give yourself a chance to? I'd say you were maybe thirty when you went to prison. The right age to try for responsibility, Mister Castle.'

He grinned a little. 'You missed it by a few years. I'm older than you think. I'm crowding forty-one.'

'Exactly the right age, Mister Castle. I pay well and I don't interfere.'

He sighed. 'Sure is a nice night, isn't it?'

Her eyes did not leave his face. For a while she had no more to say. Not until a foraging pack of coyotes sounded far northward as they sped along in search of carrion. 'At forty you have to face the future, Mister Castle.'

'Yes'm. You sound like my mother.'

Her tone lost its briskness and became softer. 'You did something for Horseshoe Liston. Will you do something for me? I know one thing about you, Mister Castle. You are a caring individual . . . Will you at least try out as rangeboss?'

He shifted in the old chair. 'How about the riders and the cook?'

'You won't have a bit of trouble. They are good men.'

'Maybe. I was an outlaw. That makes a difference with people.'

She twisted in the chair to face him fully. 'I

105

won't tell them and neither will Curtis. But if they do find out someday, by then they will already have made up their minds about you.'

He smiled in her direction. 'Did you ever lose out when you went after something, ma'm?'

She regarded him from an expressionless face for a moment before ignoring the question to make a statement. 'You like the country and the people. You are a rangeman . . . Ben; I think you need me as much as I need you . . . I don't want you to leave. You need something. You need a place to tie up and belong to.'

He stared at her so long she abruptly arose and moved to the door of the house, where she said, 'Everybody needs something, Mister Castle, we don't all find it . . . You can bed down at the bunkhouse and we'll ride to town together in the morning. Good night.'

He came up to his feet. 'Wait a minute. Why do I feel like there is something between us that's not being said?'

She opened the door. 'Good night, Mister Castle.'

He remained on the porch after she had gone inside. Finally, as he started down across the yard toward the bunkhouse, the scent of pipe-smoke reached him from over along the front of the cookhouse. He could see someone sitting over there in a tipped-back chair, and for no particular reason changed course.

The *cocinero* had been doing this for many

106

years, when the weather was good. During those years he'd had his relaxing reveries interrupted many times by riders who had come out into the yard after nightfall, so when Ben Castle strolled up, Soapy removed his pipe and pointed to an empty chair with it, then he said, 'Fine night.' He trickled smoke briefly, and said something else. 'Sound carries a hell of a distance on clear nights like this.'

Ben eyed the big older man in silence. Soapy removed the pipe and peered into its bowl. 'She made you a good offer.'

A man couldn't be accused of eavesdropping when he had not meant to eavesdrop. Ben rocked his chair back too, as he said, 'I know it's a good offer. The thing is, I've never been a rangeboss.'

'You ain't goin' to be one any longer, mister.'

Ben did not respond to what he considered a worn-out answer, so the cook spoke again. 'Tell you something, friend. She sure deserves better than she's had. I never trusted Herb, but she did, and that gave me grey hair . . . Tell you something else, partner—that son of a bitch she was married to . . .'

Ben's eyes widened in shock.

'He moved in when her paw was dyin' and she was alone and scairt . . . The best thing that happened to her was when he finished killin' himself with whisky.'

Soapy's chair came down off the wall as he

107

beat dottle from the little pipe and heaved up to his feet looking in the direction of the main-house. 'Your name is Ben? Ben, hire on as her rangeboss. I heard what she said on the porch, and it's the gospel truth: Everyone needs somethin' an' they don't always find it. She needs more help than I can give her. Good night.'

CHAPTER ELEVEN

ON THE TRAIL

Because he was not eager to get down to Kearneyville the next morning, Ben went down to the barn with the riders to help do the chores, and afterwards he trooped to the cookshack with them for breakfast.

They were ordinary range riders, not particularly talkative around someone they did not know, and well-seasoned at their trade when they watched Ben as he helped out in an effort to determine how qualified he was. But at breakfast when Soapy got the conversation going, they loosened a little.

Later, when he was out back currying the livery horse and wondering how much he was going to owe that liveryman who owned the animal, Amy Edmond came down to lean and watch for a while as she said, 'When you're finished I'd like to show you something.'

He returned to the barn with her, tossed the comb and wheat-straw brush into a box nailed to the wall which had other combs and brushes in it, then let her have the lead.

They went toward the main-house but veered off before they reached it and passed between two outbuildings walking in the direction of several old cottonwood trees inside a plot of ground which was surrounded by a wrought-iron fence high enough to keep cattle and horses out.

They passed through a small gate where morning shade speckled the ground above several stone headboards. He read the inscriptions. The first grave was that of her father. The second one was of her mother. There was another grave closer to one of the big old trees which seemed older than the others. The man buried there had been named Bowie McClintock. Amy said, 'I never knew him. He came into the country with my folks. He and two other Texans. They were drovers. My father brought four hundred head along for his seed stock. Bowie McClintock was killed breaking a wild horse. My father said he got kicked in the head.'

She turned slightly toward another grave. Ben glanced over there and read the inscription. This was where her husband had been buried.

109

Ben got an uncomfortable feeling. There were no other graves and he had seen all he cared to see. In fact more than he cared to see. He ordinarily had no reason to visit cemeteries, had not been in one in many years, and was not pleased to be in this one, although he remembered what she had said last night about showing him the graves of her parents, making some kind of implication as they had talked.

She was standing in soft-golden morning sunshine, partly in shade. 'He was a rangeman. The last one my father ever hired . . . He was the biggest mistake in my entire life.'

Ben reached to brush her arm, and jerked his head. There was no point in this. As they reached the little gate and he held it for her, she turned and smiled, then walked on through without a word.

They had covered half the distance toward the yard and she was walking at his side looking down when she said, 'If we're going to get to town and back again before dark, we'd better go now.'

He had not wanted to go down there, but right now the idea had appeal because it would probably jerk her out of the doldrums visiting that graveyard had dropped her into. He looked up and around. The riders were gone. He thought they either knew without being told what to do today, or perhaps she had already given them their orders.

110

The *cocinero* was draping wet dishtowels from a length of rope stretched across his cookhouse porch. He ignored them so hard Ben wanted to smile.

Out front of the barn Amy said, 'We'd better trail a horse with us so's you'll have something to ride back on,' then she turned and walked in the direction of the main-house, and Ben leaned on the tie-rack gazing after her. He had not said he would come back.

Over at the porch the *cocinero* had finished with his towels and was solemnly stuffing shag into a little pipe. After he had lighted up he glanced across and said, 'I can fix up a little bundle for you folks to eat on the way.'

Ben shifted slightly so he could see the older man in his wreath of bluish smoke. 'How do you always manage to be where you listen to what folks talk about?' he asked, and the cook drew up to his full, impressive height as he removed the pipe.

'Why is it my fault if folks talk when I'm around? Ben, I don't give a damn what you do. I was just offerin' to be helpful is all.'

Ben nodded, still eyeing the big, older man. He never should have said that, and if he had thought he would have known better; he had yet to be anywhere near a cow-ranch cook without encountering an irascible disposition. It seemed to go with the trade, for some damned reason. He said, 'Anything you want from

111

town?' and that took a little of the starch out of Soapy. He puffed for a moment and finally answered, speaking in a lowered voice and looking toward the main-house.

'Yeah. She don't like liquor on the place . . . A quart of panther piss. Keep it hid in your saddlebags.'

Ben straightened up. 'All right. Which horse should I saddle for her?'

Soapy looked resigned. 'Bein' a woman, she rides mostly mares. I never could understand why women like mares better'n geldings. Because they're female too, do you reckon?'

Ben had never thought about it, but he nodded anyway. 'Which horse, Soapy?'

'That blood-bay mare out back in a corral by herself . . . because when she's horsing she squeals and bites and kicks the other animals.' Soapy glared. 'Mares!' he exclaimed, and went stamping back inside his cookhouse.

Ben found the blood-bay, brought her to the barn, guessed which saddle and bridle Amy Edmond rode, and rigged the mare out. She was evidently having one of her docile days because she did not even wring her tail when he snugged up the cinch.

The livery horse did not especially want to leave his corral to enter the barn, not simply because he knew he was to be saddled and ridden, but because he was enjoying himself at the ranch.

When Amy arrived at the barn Ben was working on the third horse. She pulled on doeskin roping-gloves, eyed the mare and said, 'How did you know?'

He was leading the animals out of the barn to be mounted when he replied shortly, 'Soapy.'

He turned the stirrup for her to mount, then looked up and met her dark blue gaze. 'There's no reason for you to make this ride,' he said to her. 'I can find my way.'

She nodded her head. 'Sure you can.' She then glanced at the sun. 'We should have started earlier.'

He went over and swung up. One darned sure thing about women; if they didn't want to give a direct answer wild horses couldn't drag one out of them.

They walked a mile then loped a mile. Ben knew the territory over to the west because that was how he had got up here before. But the country was not that different over there or over here, except that they encountered several fairly large bands of cattle grazing over a couple of miles of good grass. They also passed that creek where he had bathed yesterday. A mile or so beyond it she swerved for no reason that Ben could understand, but he also swerved.

She skirted the rim of an overgrown arroyo which had trees growing down in it. He leaned to look for water down there. If it was not on the surface, then it was not very far below it because otherwise those trees and wild berry bushes would not look so healthy.

She stopped and pointed with a gloved hand. He looked for a minute, then saw it; a small circular clearing with mounded rocks in the centre. He knew what it was before she spoke.

'That's Emily's place.'

It was a grave. It looked to be fairly old. He said, 'Who was Emily?'

'A Shoshone woman. My mother took her in. The Indians had left her to die because she had smallpox. My mother got her through, and she never left. She helped raise me.'

'Why isn't she buried back at the ranch?'

The dark blue eyes came around to his face. 'That was one of the last things she asked my father not to do. She did not want to lie among only whites. She told us about this place, and this is where we buried her.'

Amy led the way past the arroyo and back westward again. Ben looped his reins and rolled a smoke. She watched him, and when he lighted up, took down a deep drag and let the smoke trickle out, she said, 'What did the riders have to say at breakfast?'

He shrugged. 'Nothing much. I guess me being there made them a little uncomfortable. But they were friendly. I'd say you have a good crew, Mrs Edmond.'

He had barely pronounced the last word than it occurred to him that she had led him into his comment. He was right. She said, 'They are for a fact, but there is no rangeboss material among them.'

He considered the distance, the golden flow of sun-brilliance, and finally the tip of his quirley. And he relented. 'All right, but if it don't work within a month or two . . .'

They discussed cattle, range conditions, the prospects for summer showers to keep the feed strong, and by the time they had rooftops in sight, he had made her laugh a couple of times.

He discovered that she was not always terse. In fact before they reached the upper end of Kearneyville he had made several discoveries about her.

She had made a few about him too. With her gaze fixed ahead she said, 'Friends, Ben?'

He smashed out the smoke and regarded her with suspicion. The last time she said that she'd asked personal questions.

When he did not respond she looked over and saw his expression. 'Friends?'

His reply was a little rueful. 'Well, I guess so—some of the time anyway.'

She laughed. He smiled at her. She looked younger when she laughed. 'Why aren't you married?' she said.

It was easier for him to answer that question than it had been to answer the one she had asked him in the kitchen last night.

'I didn't see anyone up at the Canon City

prison I figured I'd want to marry.'

Her terseness returned. 'That was only six years. What about the other thirty or so?'

'Didn't have anything. Most of the time I even rode other people's horses. On cowboy wages even an In'ian woman wouldn't have me.'

She thought about that before asking another question. 'What about your family?'

He got a little annoyed. 'Dead and buried and I don't see what any of this has got to do with me hiring out as your rangeboss.'

She retreated quickly. 'I'm sorry.'

He watched the buildings, the trees, the light traffic which was entering and leaving Kearneyville. He thought of Curtis Shelby, the friendly barman who combed his hair into a cow-lick, and the paunchy cafeman who always wore floppy old felt slippers. Finally, closer to the outskirts of Kearneyville, he said, 'Herb Oliver struck me as one of a kind.'

She agreed. 'He was. Soapy never liked him, and I never was sure the other riders did, but he knew livestock and how to manage a big ranch . . . What depressed me was learning what else he was good at . . . Did he say exactly how he was going to take over Tomahawk?'

Ben shook his head. Oliver had never come right out with how he intended to do that, but Ben Castle had met a lot of men in prison who would have answered Amy Edmond easily and

curtly about how someone like Herb Oliver
would do that.

'Ben, six or seven years ago I had a very good
offer to sell Tomahawk. Sometimes I think I
should have accepted it.'

'Why didn't you?'

'I showed you some of the reasons this
morning.'

He thought about that. Perhaps if those had
been his parents under the old trees, he would
have felt the same way, but their graves were
many miles away, he had not visited them since
heading west, and he did not have quite the
same feeling about graves she seemed to have.

'And there was another reason,' she said
softly. 'I wanted my children to grow up on
Tomahawk as I had done.'

That startled him.

'But I didn't have any children, and my
dream of what marriage was, turned out to be
childish. I expected too much, I think.'

He turned toward her, wordless and sorry for
her. She smiled. 'And now I'm too old.'

That, at least, was something he could
remark about. 'You're not too old, Amy. Well,
I don't know about children, but you're closer
to bein' a girl than you are to bein' a woman.'
He paused, reconsidered that, then said, 'Well,
when you laugh or smile, or get embarrassed,
you look no more'n maybe eighteen. But you're
the boss, and I guess that makes you a woman,

117

don't it?'

He had struggled through that, and now he reddened under her steady gaze, and finally made a little crooked smile at her. 'Hell, I never was any good with words.'

She smiled slowly, then laughed, which brought more colour to his face. 'And I also ask personal questions.'

He grinned ruefully. 'Yeah, you do that for a fact.'

'Not out of curiosity, Ben. Out of interest. When you leaned over my bed last night you scairt me half to death . . . but after I'd listened to you . . . you were different. You weren't like . . . anyone else.'

She too was struggling, but in her case the struggle was not to say too much.

They were closer to the north roadway now and a big freight outfit Ben had watched earlier was about parallel. The driver raised a thick arm in a high salute and Ben waved back.

CHAPTER TWELVE

A TALL MAN

The liveryman greeted them with a wide smile, which he might not have exhibited if Ben had come in alone, but everyone knew Amy

Edmond.

Ben apologised for keeping the horse so long, and dug into a trouser pocket for some silver coins. The liveryman hauled off the saddle and walked completely around his animal, then came over smiling. 'You're a horseman,' he said to Ben, offering the biggest compliment anyone in his business could offer. 'He looks better'n when you taken him out.'

Ben handed the lead-rope to their led-horse to a youthful hostler and asked how much he owed. The liveryman caught Amy Edmond's gaze over Ben's shoulder, and cleared his throat before mentioning a figure.

Ben blinked. 'That's too low,' he said, but the liveryman was equal to this occasion. 'Naw. Not when someone brings back a horse better'n when he took him out, mister.'

Ben counted out the money, watched the liveryman take the blood-bay mare, and turned to glance up the roadway. Amy said, 'Are you hungry?'

He wasn't. 'No ma'm. Are you?'

She lied sweetly. 'No. Then I suppose we'd better go see if Curtis is in his office.' As they walked northward on the plankwalk, she also said, 'I've known him since he came into the country. He's a shrewd man, Ben. He's an unusual lawman. He has the size and heft to go bear-hunting with a switch, but I've seen him talk more men out of being troublesome than

119

most lawmen would have bothered with.'

They passed a number of other pedestrians, and while without exception they smiled and nodded at Amy Edmond, the ones who seemed to know who Ben was looked more startled at seeing him in town than pleased about it. He sighed about that, but said nothing.

The sheriff was not at the jailhouse, but a tall, narrow-faced younger man was there, and when Ben told the tall man who he was, the close-spaced brown eyes in that narrow face brightened with a reptilian stare. The tall man ignored Amy Edmond, reached in a pocket and held forth a federal marshal's badge for Ben to see, then he pocketed the badge and swept back the right side of his coat. An ivory-handled sixgun cradled in a hand-carved black holster was visible. The tall man said, 'I've been waiting.'

Ben considered the tall man who had not mentioned his name. 'Waiting for what?'

'You.'

Ben's gaze remained fixed upon the marshal's face. 'You fellers got Ames for the robbery and killing. You got his friend Herb Oliver. That ends it.'

The tall man slowly shook his head, brilliant eyes unwaveringly fixed on Ben. 'That don't end it, Castle. You were implicated with them. Ames told us so.'

Amy gasped. Neither of the men looked

around. 'Ames is a liar,' Ben retorted. 'Who went after him and brought him back for that killing and robbery? If we were in it together do you think I'd have done that?'

The tall man did not move nor shift his gaze. He ignored Ben's question to say, 'You're a fool. You should have got on your horse and never looked back.'

Ben's astonishment was past. Now, he perhaps should have been angry. Instead he stared at the tall man with disgust. 'I had no reason to run, Marshal. It don't make sense, what you've been saying, and you didn't answer me: Why would I have gone after Bill Ames if he and I'd been together on that damned robbery?'

The roadway door opened, Sheriff Shelby walked in, halted to look from Ben to the tall lawman, then closed the door as he said, 'Amy . . . ?'

She turned on him. 'Why is Ben being accused of having been part of that killing and robbery, Curtis?'

Shelby shouldered past to his desk and eased down upon one corner of it as he replied, looking at Amy and ignoring the two men. 'It was mentioned is all, Amy.'

She came back angrily. 'Mentioned? That deputy marshal just accused Ben of being implicated and said Ames had done the implicating. Curtis, if it were true, do you think

121

for one minute Ben would have—?'

Shelby was turning as he said, 'Marshal, we discussed it. That's all. You, me, and your partner, Deputy Haskell. We decided it wasn't true.'

The tall man finally shifted his glance from Ben to Sheriff Shelby. 'You heard Bill Ames say it, Sheriff. Castle is an ex-felon who was sent to prison for stopping a stagecoach. You had one stopped west of town, money taken off it and the driver killed. What more—'

Shelby stood up. 'What the hell is wrong with you, Harrison? We went over all that before we went up to Tomahawk and brought back Oliver and Ames.'

The tall federal officer stood stiffly silent for a moment then almost hurled himself at the door and slammed out of the jailhouse office. Ben stared after the man. So did Amy. But the sheriff went over to open the door and watch the tall man's enraged progress across the roadway, then up toward the saloon. He slowly closed the door and looked from Amy to Ben before going to the chair behind his desk and sitting down. 'Crazy,' he murmured to himself. 'What got into him?'

Ben shoved back his hat. He had not wanted to come here. But now that he was here he wanted to get it over with and get out where the air was fresh again. 'What did Bill Ames say about me?' he asked the sheriff.

Shelby raised his head slightly. 'He weaseled like most of them do. First, he offered to show us where a big cache is hid, then he made up some cock-and-bull story about you organising the robbery.' Curtis Shelby shook his head and leaned forward on the desk. 'You weren't out there. I can prove that by the feller who tracked your buggy marks. When I told Ames he was a damned liar, and told him how I knew that, he started off with a fresh idea. This time he offered the federal marshals and me directions to a hideout up north where half a dozen wanted outlaws he knew in prison have been holing up between robberies.' Shelby glanced at Amy. 'If Ames ever told the truth, it hasn't been lately,' he told her dryly, then swung his attention back to Ben Castle. 'I don't like this. I didn't like the looks of it when I walked in.' He stood up. 'I can't make you do anything. There's no charge against you. But I'd take it kindly if you'd stay in here until I get back.'

Amy said, 'Where are you going?'

The big man considered her tilted face in thought, then moved around the desk toward the roadside door as he replied. 'I'm going to find the other one, the man named Haskell. Either him and Harrison have cooked up something I don't know anything about, or that tall one's crazy.'

At the door Shelby looked over Amy's head at Ben. 'Give me fifteen minutes. Stay inside.'

123

He shook his head and went out closing the door after himself.

In the sudden silence Amy and Ben exchanged a look. She said, 'I'm glad we came together.'

He nodded without seeing that that made any difference. He went to a chair, sat down and shoved his feet out. He was baffled, not because Bill Ames had tried desperately to create confusion, to sow seeds of doubts in the minds of the federal lawmen; he thought that if he had been in Bill's boots he might have tried something equally desperate, because unless Ames could distract the lawmen, they would take him away to be tried, and he would certainly be hanged this time, instead of being returned to prison.

What really puzzled Ben was that tall deputy marshal's attitude. Ben had faced angry men before, even men willing to draw on him, but this time he could not for the life of him imagine why there had been that unmistakable look of a killer on the stranger's face, because even if he had been implicated with Ames and Oliver, he would have deserved to be locked up like Ames and Oliver were—but the tall lawman had been on the verge of forcing a gunfight when the sheriff had walked in.

Amy said, 'I'm hungry.'

Ben raised his eyes. She smiled forlornly at him. He shoved up out of the chair and smiled at her. 'There is a cafe across the road.'

She passed him and sat down in the chair he had just vacated. 'I'll wait. Ben . . . why?'

'I don't know. It didn't make sense.'

'Have you ever seen that federal deputy before?'

'Not that I know of. Most likely I'd remember if I ever had.'

She sighed. 'Friends, Ben?'

He looked at her. 'All right. What is it this time?'

'I don't believe he ever saw you before either . . . He is one of those lawmen who hate outlaws. Even ones who are no longer outlaws but who once were.' Her violet eyes widened a little. 'He was going to kill you!'

Ben went to the little roadside window and leaned down. Nothing in sight looked much different from what it had an hour earlier when he and Amy had walked up here. That big freight wagon he had seen entering town from up north was pulled close to the duckboards over in front of the general store where two brawny men were off-loading crates and barrels, and sweating profusely as they worked.

Up in front of the saloon where he had first learned that Bill Ames had escaped from prison there were three drowsing horses at the rack out front.

He thought that by now Sheriff Shelby had found the other federal marshal. He hoped the tall one was with them. He turned away, lifted out his old sixgun, checked it for loads and eased it gently back into its holster. When he looked up Amy was watching him with perfectly round eyes. She said, 'Don't go out there. Let Curtis have his fifteen minutes . . . Please.'

He had not intended to go outside. If that tall man was not with his companion and the sheriff, he was probably watching the jailhouse hoping that Ben would emerge. Maybe, as the sheriff had said, the tall deputy federal lawman was indeed crazy. If he was, that must have been his reason for acting as he had.

Amy could have been right. He had encountered his share of lawmen, and although he had never run into one who had tried to shoot him, he had met several he had thought could do a thing like that without a qualm, because of their hatred for outlaws. It was certainly not unheard of for lawmen to have that kind of feeling.

He said, 'Hell,' and went over to sit on a chair beside the roadway door and gaze at Amy. She was pale, and that made her dark violet eyes look darker. He forced a smile. 'Did you ever have the feeling you were a tree stump and everyone around you had turned into dogs?'

She smiled, then laughed, and he had accomplished his purpose, which had been to shake her out of her fear. She regarded him for

126

a moment before speaking. 'You *are* different, Ben.'

'Compared to what?'

'. . . My husband . . . and two or three other men I've known, who were also interested in marrying a large cow ranch.'

He settled back, wondering how long fifteen minutes was, and looked across the room at her. 'You're a handsome woman,' he told her in an almost off-hand manner. 'I can't imagine a man having any other reason for marrying you, Amy.'

For once, she was speechless. She suddenly arose from the chair and went over to stand facing the gun-rack on the west wall with her back to him.

Someone up the roadway shouted. Ben stood up and stepped to the little window. Two men were on the boardwalk in front of the saloon. The man whose broad back was toward Ben Castle was Sheriff Shelby. The taller man in front of Shelby was the narrow-faced federal officer with the close-set, ferret-like brown eyes.

Ben could not see a gun, but he knew there was one. The tall man was speaking slowly as he drove Curtis Shelby backwards toward the roadway.

People were scattering, diving through open doorways or dragging children down into dog-trots between buildings. Those two brawny freighters over in front of the general store were standing like stones, staring northward. Then one of them lunged across through the store doorway, and his partner, who probably did not believe he had that much time, dropped behind two big oaken barrels he and his partner had unloaded and which nearly blocked the sidewalk. As large as the freighter was, one barrel would not have protected him, and even two barrels barely did.

Two riders coming up through town from the south end continued to walk their horses along until they saw people running for cover, then they drew rein, stared for a moment, and without a word passing between them they both whirled to their left and drove in their spurs. The startled horses did not come down short of eight feet, both racing toward a little sideroad on the east side of Main Street.

Ben pulled back and said, 'Amy; don't leave this room. You hear me? Stay here no matter what.'

He was moving toward the door with his right hand low and back a little, near the handle of his sixgun, when she whirled and said, 'Ben! What is it!'

He had the door-latch in his left hand and answered without looking back. 'Shelby and that snake-eyed one. Up in front of the saloon.'

'Ben! Don't open the door!'

He was drawing it inward carefully and slowly and ignored her. She stood transfixed as he got the door wide enough to step through. Then she swung back toward the rack, fumbled at the loose chain which ran through the trigger-guards of the rifles, shotguns and carbines on the rack, and, as he stepped out into the brilliant afternoon sunglare, she clawed frantically to get a gun free.

CHAPTER THIRTEEN

WITH DUSK COMING

The sun was on the west side of town, which provided shadows under the overhangs upon that side of the road. From the edge of the plankwalk on across to the east side, there was sunlight.

Ben stood completely still in the shadows. The tall federal lawman had Curtis Shelby backed nearly to the centre of the roadway. Shelby spoke once. Ben could see his lips moving but could hear nothing. The tall man answered, then continued to speak, and although Ben still could not see the gun because the sheriff blocked the view, he could see the tall man's face, and it was twisted and mottled and sweaty.

There was no sign of the other federal deputy marshal. In fact the roadway was completely empty from one end of Kearneyville to the other end. That big freighter behind the casks had seen Ben come out of the jailhouse and was staring as though he wanted to yell a warning. Ben ignored him, and everything else except those slowly moving men out in the roadway.

He was not a gunfighter. Like most rangemen, he had killed time in line-camps and at other boring chores practising with his weapons, but he was probably no better than average at drawing. His accuracy was good enough. A man could not shoot up a dozen boxes of shells aiming at tree-knots and cans set atop rocks without becoming fairly accurate.

He looked for the second lawman, without knowing whether he would be crouching somewhere to back his companion's play or not, but he did not see the man. He did not see anyone else but the tall lawman, Curtis Shelby, and that crouching freighter behind the barrels.

He estimated the distance, then carefully drew his Colt and cocked it, took down a big breath and moved out of the shadows into the sunlight at the edge of the duckboards.

The tall man saw him at once. His step faltered for a second, then he snarled something at Curtis Shelby and shifted slightly so that Shelby's broad back would be even more between himself and Ben Castle.

He let the sheriff continue to retreat several more steps, his eyes fixed upon the man in front with the gun, but the marshal stopped moving. He did not want Shelby close enough to jump him.

Ben counted the steps Shelby took, watched the distance widen until he thought he would not hit the sheriff, and started to raise the cocked Colt.

What followed seemed not to happen fast. It seemed to take a very long time, and in Ben's mind everything occurred slowly. The tall man took one rearward step and swung his gun-fist.

Ben's finger was tightening inside the trigger-guard when the lawman fired. Something tugged forcefully at Ben Castle's shirt on the left side as he fired back. He missed, perhaps because whatever had tugged at him had made him move. He hauled back the hammer, and this time he stepped sideways in the direction of the man behind the oak barrels.

The lawman took a wide stance this time as he fired. Wood snapped to Ben's right and the crouching freighter squawked as coal oil sprayed his face and shirtfront.

Ben saw the tall man's hand moving to haul back the dog for his third shot. He had a couple of seconds to aim. He held his breath, steadied up his grip and pulled the trigger.

The tall man buckled over, his handgun went off flinging dirt into the air, and as Ben pulled the hammer back for his next shot, Curtis Shelby launched himself forward and caught the tall lawman alongside the head with a ham-sized fist, dropping him in a heap.

Ben continued to aim up the roadway. Behind him on the east plankwalk that freighter scrambled from behind the broken barrel and dove past the doorway of the general store.

Across the road in deepening shadows, Amy Edmond was leaning with her left hand gripping an overhang upright with a Winchester saddlegun barrel resting across it. Her head was low, the gunstock was snugged back into the curve of her shoulder.

Ben heard a gruff voice and faced forward again. Sheriff Shelby was on one knee, looking back. 'Put up the gun,' he told Ben Castle.

Ben obeyed, and considered the sheriff for a moment before he said, 'That was a damn fool thing to do, jumping him like that.'

He walked up there. Behind him, down near that little easterly sideroad, two heads peered around a corner where the pair of range riders had fled, and in the doorway of the blacksmith shop a muscular older man was wiping both hands on a greasy rag and nodding his head up and down as though he agreed with what had happened.

Ben halted and looked downward. The tall man was alive, but blood was pumping where Ben's last slug had struck him. He asked Sheriff Shelby where the other one was and got a gruff answer as the sheriff tried to stop the bleeding

132

with a blue bandana.

'In the saloon. We tried to talk sense to him. He hit his partner over the head and backed me out into the roadway . . . Go fetch the doctor.'

Ben did not move. The blood was slowing. It stopped flowing while Ben watched. There was no point in getting a doctor.

He looked up as several men walked forth to stand staring. One of them was that blacksmith he had met at the cafe a week or so back. Another one was the pasty-faced, friendly barman who combed his hair into a cow-lick. The barman was pale and worried, but the blacksmith looked straight at Ben as he said, 'I'm glad you come through it alive.'

Sheriff Shelby got heavily to his feet mopping his hands and looking at the corpse. 'I never heard of anything like it,' he muttered to himself. 'Never.' He turned slowly, but Ben was already walking back down in the direction of the jailhouse. The blacksmith said, 'Curtis, you're a lucky son of a gun. You owe that feller.'

Instead of agreeing Selby said, 'Couple of you boys lend me a hand and we'll take him out back to Doc's embalming shed.'

Amy was in the office waiting when Ben arrived. The Winchester had not been replaced in the rack but was lying casually upon the desk where she had put it, and the rubbery knees which were threatening to let her fall held up

133

until she reached a chair.

Ben met her gaze and let out a long breath. Looking past him to the roadway, Amy saw people running northward where moments earlier the roadway had been totally empty. She said, 'Is he dead?'

Ben nodded. 'Yeah . . . I guess Shelby was right. He told me he met them both at the saloon, and that he and the other marshal tried to talk sense to Harrison . . . He hit the other marshal over the head, then started backing Shelby into the roadway . . . Crazy, Amy.' He went over to lean near her chair looking down. 'You ready to head home?'

She nodded but did not move in the chair. There were still pedestrians hastening up the roadway, and a large man wearing a brand-new checkered flannel shirt was standing over in front of the general store with two other men. One of them she would have known if his back had been to her. His name was Abe Dent and he owned the general store where the Tomahawk outfit had had an account for twenty-five years. Abe Dent was angrily waving his arms and bitterly complaining that all that spilled coal oil was a fire hazard, and that someone had ought to shovel dirt over it, or do something anyway, before it caught fire and destroyed all of Kearneyville.

The two big freighters were looking at Abe Dent like he was out of his head, especially the

134

one wearing the new shirt because his other shirt had been drenched by coal oil. This man finally spat into roadway dust and turned on his heel walking in the direction of the saloon. He was thirty-eight years old, had freighted for twenty of those years in all kinds of abominable weather, had faced down highwaymen, drunken cowboys and even a few redskins, but he had never gone through a day like this one— and all that damned idiot of a storekeeper could talk about was shovelling dirt over some spilled coal oil.

Ben went to lean in the doorway. Sheriff Shelby was approaching in long steps. His shirt-front was dark with sweat and his expression was sombrely bleak. Ben moved aside so the sheriff could walk in. He looked from Ben to Amy, went to a chair and dropped down, hard. When neither of them spoke, he finally said, 'Crazy as hell. Haskell was telling me up at the shed out back of Doc's place, that Harrison has been getting more violent for the past year.' Shelby raised his head. 'Ben . . . thanks.'

Castle nodded and remained silent.

Amy finally pushed out of the chair. Her colour was returning. She said, 'Now what?' to the lawman, and he wagged his head and leaned to arise. 'Nothing, I guess, Amy. You got anything in mind?'

'We're going home, Curtis.'

He finally stood up. 'I had no idea, Amy.'

Ben straightened up off the wall. 'You got Ames. That'll even things up a little for Liston. You got Herb Oliver. I guess what he didn't do was maybe worse than what he and Bill Ames did to Horseshoe Liston . . . And you got a dead federal lawman. Sheriff, as far as I'm concerned, that ends it. I'll be out at Tomahawk if you want to see me, but I'm not coming back to Kearneyville for a damned year, unless it's life and death.'

He let Amy precede him out into the widening shadows of late afternoon. Down at the livery barn when the hostler went after their horses and the proprietor came out looking breathless and incapable of thinking of which words to use, Ben spiked whatever he might have said by taking Amy by the arm down with him while he helped the hostler saddle their animals.

They did not ride up the main roadway, but left town by a shadowed back-alley. When they passed a dilapidated-looking old buggy shed which had been converted into the local doctor's embalming shed, several curious townmen craned at them, but said nothing.

North of town where a faint, late-day groundswell breeze brought the smell of open country to them, Ben fished for his makings and rolled a cigarette while his Tomahawk horse plodded along beside Amy's mount with the reins swinging.

He turned and said, 'I told you not to come with me today.'

She thought about that for a moment before replying. 'I'm glad I did, Ben.'

He exhaled blue smoke. 'Did you take that carbine from the wall rack?'

'Yes.'

'It probably wasn't loaded.'

'I loaded it . . . I dropped ten for every one I shoved into the magazine . . . I've never been so afraid in my life.'

He watched the mountains retreating into the settling, far dusk. 'I'll tell you something, Amy. I was pretty darned scairt too.' He lipped the quirley and let it die without drawing on it. 'I'll tell you something else: I made a hell of a bad start in this territory.'

That stung her. 'Bad start! Ben Castle, by the end of the week they'll have made you into a hero.'

He did not reply to that, but when they had loped a couple of miles and were slackening to a walk again, he looked over at her. 'Amy . . . Did your paw wish you'd been a boy?'

She blinked at him. 'Well. Yes he did.'

Ben smiled slightly. 'He should have been around today. If you'd been a man you couldn't have done any better. Maybe you wouldn't even have done as well.'

She matched his small grin. 'My knees

137

turned to water,' she told him, then changed the subject, her tone of voice getting brisk. 'First thing in the morning I'll ride out with you. Show you where the salt logs are and where the cattle drink, and as much more as we can see in one day. The men have plenty to do without you for a day or two . . . Ben?'

'Yes'm.'

'. . . Don't call me that.'

'What then? Not Amy; that wouldn't sound right in front of the hired hands. Mrs Edmond?'

She set her jaw. 'Amy. And what I was going to say was: Where is your horse?'

'I don't own one. I rode a stagecoach down here. I haven't owned a horse in—.'

'Six years,' she exclaimed. 'Ben, I know six years is a long time, but that particular six years is past and gone.'

He silently agreed with that, because he had decided not to dwell upon it on the coach ride to Kearneyville. He had seen what resentment and bitterness could do to men. 'Past and gone,' he murmured, looking for rooftops. 'You don't have to show me the range, Amy. I can ride with the men and in time I'll get to know it well enough.'

She too was looking dead ahead when she replied. 'I know I don't have to. I want to . . . Soapy goes to town for supplies once a month with the wagon. If he knew what sizes you wear

138

in shirts and britches and all . . .'

Ben groaned under his breath. He had forgotten to fetch back the *cocinero*'s quart of whisky. 'When is he going?' he asked.

'In a week or so. He lets me know when he's low on flour and so forth. Why?'

'Because I left some personal stuff at the roominghouse and he could pick it up for me.'

'He can make the trip tomorrow,' she said, and squinted a little. 'He comes back half drunk every blessed time . . . Whisky is poison.'

He looked over at her profile, saw the pain, and looked toward the buildings again. Several men were in the yard, but oncoming dusk obscured everything about them except the fact that they were moving.

As she reined around between the distant little cemetery and her large main-house, she said, 'I didn't mean whisky had to be poison . . . I meant it is to some people.'

He smiled to himself. 'Never been much of a drinker, Amy, but now and then it helps.'

'I'll make us some supper at the house, Ben.'

'Naw,' he replied, watching the porch of the cookhouse until he saw the *cocinero* come out and stand there looking expectant. 'I'll bed down at the bunkhouse, Amy. I'd kind of like to go down to the creek and have another bath, and maybe to sit in on a bunkhouse poker session—if they get one going after work. Then

139

I'd sort of like to go out and maybe watch the moon come up . . . Amy, I never killed a man before.'

She slackened the reins as they started to cross toward the barn where two riders were leaning, watching and waiting. 'In the morning, then, Ben. Right after breakfast.'

CHAPTER FOURTEEN

BACK AT TOMAHAWK

For two bits the *cocinero* cut Ben's hair, but not happily since Ben had not brought his bottle of pop-skull back from town, although his mood improved considerably when in mitigation Ben explained that Soapy would be sent to town tomorrow. He did not mention the events in Kearneyville which had made him forget the whisky. Soapy would no doubt hear all about them at the Kearneyville saloon.

Nor did he mention the shoot-out at the bunkhouse poker game, but for some reason the riders seemed to suspect Ben Castle and their employer had not ridden down there just because of the scenery and pleasant weather. Nothing was said, though. The riders were discreet men, professionals at their trade; all they expected from a hired man, even a new rangeboss, was that he carry his end of things.

But neither did they have any idea the stranger named Castle had been offered Herb Oliver's job, and had accepted the offer. One discovery they made though, was that Ben Castle was a very good poker player. He won two dollars, which was a fair-sized pot for one night's play, and when they were breaking it up, getting coffee and rolling smokes, a young cowboy with a good-natured smile inadvertently touched a nerve when he kidded Ben about being an expert and said, 'I had an uncle back in Kansas who got sent to prison for stealin' horses. When he come back a few years later, wasn't a man in our town who could beat him at poker. I heard him tell my paw one time that one thing a man got real good at in prison, was cards.'

One of the other man went down to the barn to look around before retiring. The others winked about that, 'Charley,' one man explained to Ben, 'always does that. Every blessed night summer or winter. He never finds anything wrong, but he's got to go look anyway.'

Ben was out front rolling a smoke when Charley returned and smilingly reported that the horses were bedded down. He stopped for a moment to enjoy the warm, softly-lighted summer night, breathed deeply a few times then glanced around when Ben lighted up. 'I

141

never worked for a lady-owner before,' he confided. 'But I got to say, she's right decent.'

Ben nodded about that. He had arrived at the same conclusion long ago, and he had not as yet put in one full day in her employ.

Charley relaxed and opened up a little more. 'Her husband though . . . I was workin' here when they got married.'

Ben eyed the stocky, shorter man. 'What kind of feller was he?'

Charley had to ruminate a little before answering. 'I was raised to say nothin' about folks if it wasn't nice.' He grinned and did not say another word.

Ben smiled. 'I sort of gathered he was about like you just didn't say he was.'

Charley was tickled by that and laughed. 'We been wondering about Herb and Bill.'

'Wondering what?'

'Well; someone said you was probably a lawman on their trail.'

'Naw. I wouldn't be much of a lawman. But I wanted Bill Ames for a killing.'

'Yeah? Who'd he kill?'

'Remember hearing about that payroll-stage that got robbed west of Kearneyville?'

Charley sobered quickly. 'That driver?'

'Yeah.'

Charley said, 'We figured it had to be a real big robbery when Lewis and Dan picked that big bag out of the coal over at the shoeing shed

142

. . . But until we seen 'em take Herb and Bill away we could only guess, and even afterwards no one figured it was that robbery and killing.'

Castle said, 'It was,' and stamped out his cigarette. 'Tell me something, Charley: What kind of a foreman was Oliver?'

Again the cowboy ruminated before replying. Evidently that ethical concept of not speaking evil about people had been drilled deeply into him.

Ben began a slow smile, which Charley saw and understood. He said, 'Well sir, I'll put it this way: I'm near forty year old an' I've worked around a lot in my time, sometimes for real decent bosses, sometimes for miserable ones, but only once did I ever work for one that I just couldn't never really like.'

They looked at each other briefly, and Ben chuckled. He said, 'I'm going out back to look in on the horses. Good night.'

Charley watched Ben stroll in the direction of the corrals, sighed and went inside where the men were discussing Bill Ames, Herb Oliver, and the new man named Castle.

There was a fair-sized moon and a seemingly endless rash of stars. Ben halted at the horse-corral and looked at the using animals inside. They were drowsing and showed no interest in his presence.

He had vivid memories of what had happened in the Kearneyville roadway, and

143

although his conscience did not bother him at all, he nevertheless regretted what he had done down there. Killing someone was not anything he had thought much about over the years, mainly because there had been very few times in his life when it had seemed necessary, and he had managed to get out of those instances without having to use his gun.

He knew of a certainty that as long as he lived he would never forget the face of the deputy U.S. marshal. It might be, as an old sheepman had once told him in Wyoming, that once a man kills someone, a little bit of him dies along with his victim.

He also recognised the danger, and the futility, of dwelling upon a killing. It could not be undone, and it probably could not be forgotten, but it could be put so far back in the recesses of a man's mind that the passage of time would pretty well take care of it.

He thought about Ames and the laughs, poker sessions, and exchanged confidences they had shared in prison. He did not believe Bill Ames was going to walk away this time, or go back to prison. He was saddened by that too.

A mammy cow started bawling in the distance and Ben listened to determine whether she was upset about nearby predators, perhaps after a baby calf, or just unable to locate her offspring. It was not the frantic sound wet cows made, so he decided her youngster had decided

144

to go exploring by moonlight, to her distress and disapproval.

Tomahawk was a very large outfit. He did not know how large, but he had been a rangeman most of his life, and had the instinct about such things that rangemen develop.

It was going into the second generation, which meant the land was clear and the cattle were too. First-generation stockmen worked their hearts out; second generation ones inherited the fruit of all that cussing, sweating, broken bones and whatnot. Amy was good at managing. Instinct told him that too. But he had a typical rangeman's feelings about a woman operating a livestock ranch. Womenfolk weren't supposed to be at marking-grounds where men got stomped and butted, and bruised, and turned the air blue with their profanity.

There was something else: Amy was terse. He had never encountered that in a woman before. He had known disagreeable ones, conniving ones, and a few downright dishonest ones.

The old cow must have located her errant offspring because she stopped her caterwauling. He turned, settled his back against corral stringers and gazed around the yard. Without having seen many Tomahawk cattle up close, he knew they would be in good flesh and culled down to where there would be few gummers to haphazardly calve in springtime. The livestock would be strong and productive, exactly as the log buildings were well-maintained and strictly functional. A man wanted to work for an outfit he could be proud of.

A horse squealed and he turned, found the blood-bay mare, and gently wagged his head. Darned animal was peevishly nipping the flanks of the drowsing geldings. Sure as God had made green apples she was coming into season. There were only a few things, like maybe biting dogs and rattlesnakes, which were more annoying than a damned horsing mare.

He watched a big, rawboned bay gelding pin his ears back and whale away, heard the solid sound of hooves striking the mare's ribs, and smiled because the mare went off by herself leaving the other animals at peace. The next time Amy annoyed him he was going to light into her about riding that damned mare.

Someone blew out the bunkhouse lamp, and there was a noticeable coolness coming into the night, so Ben strolled back toward the bunkhouse. When he entered it was as dark as the inside of a boot, and someone had chunked a wedge of wood into the stove to keep the building warm through the night.

He took an empty bunk, and within five minutes was sleeping like a log.

When he opened his eyes the bunkhouse was cool and someone was over in front of the stove

146

in his long-john underwear shoving in paper and kindling. Outside, the stillness was deafeningly deep.

Ben rolled out, pulled on his britches and boots then headed out back to wash. Charley came out looking like a tousle-headed ghost in boots and long-johns. They exchanged grunts meant to be greetings, and as Charley waited for Ben to finish with the wash-pan, soap and old roller towel, he stepped to the edge of the little rear porch, cleared his pipes, lustily spat, then began to scratch as he said, 'She'll send us out to mind first-calf heifers today.' He turned from admiring the softly fading night. 'I been here so long I can dang near read her mind. She'll maybe pair you off with one of us other fellers so's you can get an idea of the range and all.'

Ben was towelling off when he said, 'You're sure?'

Charley was positive. 'I told you—I been here long enough to know.'

Ben flung away the water and stepped clear so that Charley could start his ablutions. He said, 'Charley, she's a fine-looking woman.'

Charley did not look up from splashing water but he answered shortly. 'Ben, don't you make that mistake. I've seen them come and go since her husband died. She's downright handsome for a fact, but she's got a heart with a big Tomahawk brand right in the centre of it. That's all she's interested in. Don't make the

147

mistake them other fellers made. She can put you on ice with one look, then fire you for thinkin' otherwise.'

Ben was interested. 'Is that a fact?'

Charley was groping for the roller towel with both eyes squeezed tight when he answered. 'Take my word for it. Just do your work, draw your pay, and don't make cow-eyes at her or you'll be riding down the trail wondering what happened.'

The cook beat his triangle over on the porch of his building before the sky had brightened very much and everyone trooped over to be fed. Soapy seemed agitated about something. Ben thought he knew what it was, and after they had eaten and everyone had left, he stood in the doorway to tell Soapy what he was to fetch back with him from town, and Soapy nodded so fervently that Ben privately thought he would probably forget everything once he got down to Kearneyville where he could take on a load of Taos lightning.

The riders were bringing in using horses when Ben reached the barn. Nothing was said as the men went through a routine they had grown up with, and which most of them would be following long after their hair was grey.

Amy appeared with the first streaks of new-day light. The men looked soberly up from their work. She was booted to ride. She almost never rode out with them in the morning, unless there was a specific and critical need for her to do it.

Ben left the barn to bring in the blood-bay mare. No one heeded his departure but when he returned they looked owlishly at him.

Charley cleared his throat and reached for the flank cinch while he watched poker-faced Ben Castle lead the mare to a pole then go after Amy's outfit.

Except for one thing, Charley would have assumed the new man was just buttering up to the boss. The one thing was that Ben had brought in the mare and was now saddling her without having been told to do any of it, although Amy Edmond was standing there watching as she drew on her riding gloves.

Charley began to redden. The new man had known she was going out with them this morning, and Charley had gone to great lengths to prove how much he knew about her—and all the while that damned poker-winning, laconic son of a bitch had known better.

The riders led their horses out front to mount them. The horse Ben had saddled for himself was still standing tied in the barn and he made no move to lead him out. Amy took the reins to her mare, and also stood back in the barn as she looked into the brightening, cold yard.

'I think some of the bulls are in the mud,' she said to them. 'If you find them and they're sore-footed, drive them on in for doctoring. If

149

they're all right, push them out to the cows.'

Charley swung up, pulled his hat savagely down in front, aligned his reins and refused to look back down there where Ben was standing with his reins in hand, waiting for them to leave.

That danged poker-player had made a fool of him. He urged the horse into a walk, furious at having been proven so wrong, even down to what she would tell them to do today.

As they left the yard Ben smiled a little, watching Charley head out with a very stiff back. When Amy turned to ask if he was ready to ride, he was still watching Charley's back. He nodded without mentioning to her what had made him grin.

Soapy was waiting on the cookshack porch. When Ben and Amy went past he called to her. 'You got a list from the main-house?'

She did not have. 'No. Get what you need, Soapy . . . And Soapy . . . !'

He threw up a big hand. 'Miz' Edmond!'

She did not say what else she had been about to say to him. He smiled, nodded, and disappeared down in the direction of the wagon shed. She looked straight ahead, where the riders were loping steadily, widening the distance.

Ben chuckled.

She turned on him. 'Soapy will come back glassy-eyed. If it wasn't that the horses know

150

their way home, he'd end up ten miles from here asleep beneath a shade-tree with the horses grazing along with the wagon behind them! It's not a laughing matter!'

Ben neither commented nor doubted but that she had spoken the truth. The twinkle remained in his eyes though.

CHAPTER FIFTEEN

THE BLOOD BAY MARE

Ben had been right, it was indeed a large cow outfit. She used little hills to point out where the boundaries were, and even that did not specifically delineate anything except a general direction, because the boundaries she mentioned were many miles from where they sat while she talked.

They skirted some low foothills to the north. She owned the land all the way to the rim of the northern mountains, all useless land to a stockman. 'Good for firewood,' she said. 'Every autumn two wagons stripped to running gear go up there and bring out our winter wood.'

He nodded, lit a smoke, and said very little as they loped over brilliantly lighted rolling grassland. She showed him the three main arroyos which bisected Tomahawk, each with a

151

spring or a running creek at the bottom of it. He finally said, 'Who laid it out?'

'My father.'

Ben nodded his head. 'He was a stockman.'

She agreed. 'One of the best, Ben. There were one or two other outfits in the country when he arrived, but he was the one who rode over every yard of the land he wanted, then filed on it. The others just ran cattle over it and assumed it would always be open to them.'

He looked at her. 'A man can't be real popular with the neighbours doing something like that.'

She agreed again. 'He wasn't. Not until he'd helped them battle grass fires set by the Indians, and a dozen other disasters . . . Time does things for people, Ben. Before he died he had made friends just about everywhere. But he was still a hard and practical man.' She turned toward him. 'You remind me of him, in some ways.'

He let that lie, changed the subject when he saw dust from running horses, and she squinted a long time before saying, 'Mustangs. Most ranchers shoot them. Tomahawk has enough land and grass.' She turned again. 'Did you ever trap wild horses?'

He had. 'Yes, but only because I couldn't get hired on. It's a hard way to serve the Lord, Amy . . . Charley is a good man.'

She blinked. 'What does Charley have to do

with wild horses?'

'Nothing. He warned me not to make cow-eyes at you.'

She stared.

Ben met her gaze with a twinkle. 'If I like Tomahawk, Charley said, don't make cow-eyes or you'll fire me real fast.'

' . . . Have you made cow-eyes at me?'

He stroked his chin and squinted, watching that distant, thinning dust. 'I don't think so. Well; maybe in the sheriff's office yesterday when you were going to use a Winchester to help me.'

She continued to look at him. Eventually she said, 'Your kind of humour requires getting used to, doesn't it?'

He laughed. 'Maybe . . . Anyway, I never figured it was me making cow-eyes.'

She straightened in the saddle, colour darkened her cheeks, she abruptly put her horse into a lope and as he came along behind her she seemed to be heading for a grove of distant oaks.

By the time she had got the run out of her system they were nearing oak-shade. Ben saw round depressions in the grass, barely discernible but noticeable to anyone approaching the trees in broad daylight. When she halted he said, 'In'ian camp.'

'There are a lot of these places on the ranch,' she replied. 'There are some burial grounds too.' She hesitated, then moved deeper into the shade as she said, 'It's sad, isn't it?'

He understood what she meant. 'Yes. Have you ever been around Albuquerque or Taos or Laramie?'

'No. Why?'

'That's where it hits you hardest. They hang around on the outskirts in dirty, ragged old clothes folks have thrown out, drinking and stealing. Sometimes getting into drunken fights and killing each other.'

She dismounted and led her horse among the oaks to be tied. When he came up alongside and stepped down she said, 'I told you how my father fed them . . . I wish you had known him. You two really are alike.'

He leaned on the saddle-seat gazing over at her. Was that it? Was that why she had seemed to want him to stay; was that why she had taken that Winchester out into the roadway to help him? Was that why she had not once acted as though if he did indeed make cow-eyes at her, she would not be angered?

She met his gaze briefly, then walked over to one of the trees and turned as she dropped her hat into the grass and met his gaze across the slight distance. 'What is it?' she asked.

He straightened up off the horse, loosened the cinch and thought about how to answer her. In the end he did not answer, but walked over beside her and sank down in the grass cross-legged like an Indian, and pulled a stalk to chew on. She watched, then also sat down in the grass, and when he raised his eyes she said, 'What is it?'

'We're not covering much ground. The ranch don't end here, does it?'

She did not drop her eyes. 'No. Not for twelve more miles to the west . . . Were you remembering yesterday?'

'No. I learned a few years back to put bad things deep back in your mind and don't think about them. I'm sorry that happened, but it did, and it's over, and maybe in a short while I'll have it shoved back there.' He tossed the grass stalk away. 'You miss your father, don't you?'

Amy Edmond had good intuition, but she also had something else; an ability to see beyond the intuition. 'I said you reminded me of him. You do. But that's an accident, I guess, and it doesn't go any farther than that. I'm not looking for him in someone else.'

'That's good because you'd never find him in another man . . . Amy, about this foreman's job . . .'

'Yes?'

He looked for another grass stalk, found one, pulled it and peeled off the loose shards with her watching everything he did. She said, 'I wish you wouldn't do that. Lead up to something, then not say anything.'

155

He looked over at her. 'Amy . . . I don't think this is going to work.'

She seemed to catch her breath for a moment. 'Why not?'

'Well . . . a rangeboss does his work as a rangeboss and he don't think about other things.'

She waited.

He got rid of that stalk too. 'I think about you a lot,' he told her, looking steadily at the scuffed toes of his boots. 'You see what I'm saying?'

'No.'

His head came up. She knew exactly what he was stumbling around about. 'I think you do.'

She coloured a little. 'Cow-eyes?'

He nodded; for a moment they looked at one another, and then as though they had rehearsed this, they both started laughing at the same time. When the laughter stopped she said, 'Do you have a lot of experience making cow-eyes, Ben?'

He did not have. 'Only what the other fellers have told me, mostly.'

'I didn't think you had . . . That's why I—I don't want to have to explain something to you.'

'Explain what?'

She looked exasperated. 'You must be a good rangeman. You're thick enough in the head to be a good one, Ben.'

He thought about that for a while. 'I never told anyone I was a world-beater.'

She reached impulsively and touched his hand. 'I'm sorry. Terribly sorry. I didn't mean to say that . . . I . . . Ben . . . Friends?'

'Sure, Amy.'

'I . . . the night you brought Bill and Herb to the house, and I listened to you and looked at you . . .'

'Yeah. I reminded you of your paw.'

Her eyes flashed. 'I'm having a hard enough time. And that wasn't fair. No! You didn't remind me of him. You . . . I liked you. You were quiet-talking and practical, a calm, sensible man, and I liked you.'

He thought back to that night, and how he had looked; dirty, unshaven, sunken-eyed. Then he thought about something else. 'Amy,' he said, speaking slowly. 'How the hell can I be your rangeboss . . . and get the colleywobbles every time you walk past, or smile, or even do something plumb ordinary like pulling on your gloves?'

She smoothed the riding skirt over her knees with considerable care. 'You hired on, remember?'

'Yes, but—'

'Will you let things take their course? Be the rangeboss . . . just let things take their course. Please, Ben?'

He thought about that too for a while, before

responding.

'I have a feeling before it's over with you'll fire me. But all right . . . Things can take their course.'

'Fire you for making cow-eyes at me?' She stopped smoothing the riding skirt. 'I don't think so.' After their eyes met and held for a moment she sprang up. 'Some other time we can ride over the rest of it.'

He arose and went over to tighten her mare's cinch. The mare wrung her tail, pinned back her ears and bared her teeth as she swung her head. Ben caught her on the tip of the nose with a fist. The mare was so startled she straightened up and did not move.

Ben said, 'Amy, I'm not going to ride out with you again as long as you are on this danged idiot of a horse!'

She said, 'Yes, Ben.'

He was as startled as the mare had been, and looked narrowly to see if she was being sarcastic. She wasn't, and he felt a little embarrassed for having talked to her like that. But he did not apologise, and as they turned southward in the direction of the home-place, she said, 'I'll turn her out tomorrow. Will you pick out a gelding for me?'

He felt worse. If there was one thing he had not expected Amy Edmond to do, it was to capitulate like this, and it made him feel like a bully. He said, 'Maybe we could pick one out together?'

She smiled at him. 'I'd like that.'

As he rode beside her he thought of Charley and the other riders, and what they were going to say.

The hell with them!

Photoset, printed and bound in Great Britain by
REDWOOD BURN LIMITED, Trowbridge, Wiltshire